George Makepeace Towle

Certain men of mark

Studies of living celebrities

George Makepeace Towle

Certain men of mark
Studies of living celebrities

ISBN/EAN: 9783337109110

Printed in Europe, USA, Canada, Australia, Japan

Cover: Foto ©Andreas Hilbeck / pixelio.de

More available books at **www.hansebooks.com**

CERTAIN MEN OF MARK:

Studies of Living Celebrities.

BY

GEORGE MAKEPEACE TOWLE.

BOSTON:
ROBERTS BROTHERS.
1880.

UNIVERSITY PRESS:
JOHN WILSON AND SON, CAMBRIDGE.

CONTENTS.

CERTAIN MEN OF MARK.

I.

GLADSTONE.[1]

THE lobbies of the Lords and Commons, in the Parliament Palace at Westminster, are free for every one to enter; and there it is that one may, any day during the parliamentary session, meet the statesmen of England, as it were,

[1] The author having sent a copy of this sketch to Mr. Gladstone, received from him the following reply:—

"LONDON, *April* 21, '80.

"DEAR SIR,—I have now read the article so kindly sent me twice over, and I congratulate you as an author on a paper of so much ability and so much discernment.

"In its praise it is far too liberal. To only one of the items set down on the other side do I take any exception. I really do not admit myself to have been a bad follower. There never was any opposition between Lord Hartington and myself on the Public Worship Bill. On the Eastern Question I was too deeply committed by antecedent action, as well as by conviction, to be simply obedient; for which, however, on various occasions, I made great efforts.

"I remain, dear sir,
"Your faithful and obedient,
"W. E. GLADSTONE."

tête-à-tête. It is interesting to observe eminent
men from a near point of view, and at moments
when they are " off duty; " and in the lobbies,
during the half hour before the two Houses are
called to order, the members stand about, chat
with a friend here and a constituent there, and
relax, if ever, their official dignity in social con-
verse.

It was in the lobby of the Commons that,
some fifteen years ago, I first saw Mr. Gladstone.
He was then in the full prime of life, being about
fifty-five years of age. He had already won a
degree of political renown only less than the
highest. At that time he was Chancellor of
the Exchequer in Lord Palmerston's cabinet;
and, next to Lord Palmerston, was the most
distinguished member of the popular House.
He had been a member of parliament thirty-
three years; and his career there, at least as far
as reputation was concerned, had been a tri-
umphal progress, ever and steadily advancing.
No one doubted that at some day not far distant
Mr. Gladstone would be summoned to assume
the post of Prime Minister.

A glance sufficed to recognize him. His photographs peered at the passer-by from every

bookstore and print shop in London; and no one could have seen them without taking note of the very remarkable, expressive, intense features they discovered. But there was something about Mr. Gladstone as he stood there, gravely talking with two gentlemen who listened to him with every outward sign of respect, which the photographs had not disclosed. There was a certain plainness, almost rusticity, of dress and external appearance; a thick-set, farmer-like body, far from graceful; a certain negligence of attire and toilet and manner, and simple gravity of bearing, which one had not expected to see in the brilliant and eloquent scholar who had so often thrilled the House, and, through the medium of the press, the world. But after the first superficial glance, when you raised your eyes to the face and head, and observed the features, you soon found the man's character reflected there. The not very large, but brilliant, earnest, burning eyes; the retreating, but nobly shaped forehead; the very un-English swarthy complexion; the firm, thin mouth, to which every line lent new expressiveness; the square-set jaw, and bold straight nose; the spirit and warmth that glowed in the whole countenance

betokened a mind and soul alike lofty, zealous,
and intense.

Never once did the slightest smile cross those
almost grim features; and the contrast between
this grimness of expression, and the sweet, silvery voice, the tones of which now and then
reached my ear, was very striking. Mr. Gladstone's smiles, indeed, are very few and slight.
He has always been too dead-in-earnest; and
dead-in-earnestness has stamped itself on his
face, as it has throughout the record of his public career.

Not many evenings after, I was fortunate
enough to see Mr. Gladstone on another scene,
and in a new aspect. A great debate was proceeding in the House of Commons, on the usually dry subject of Supply. Mr. Gladstone had,
as Chancellor of the Exchequer, brought in a
Budget, some features of which had aroused the
hostility of certain attacked interests. Among
other items he had proposed, for the first time,
to tax the great public charities of England.
Such institutions as Bartholomew and Christ's
Hospitals had before been exempt from taxa-
tion, as being devoted to purposes of benevolence. They had now grown, however, to be

rich and powerful corporations; and Mr. Gladstone declared that they should aid in support-
ing the expenses of the country. The proposal
aroused great indignation, especially among the
established clergy, who to a large extent con-
trolled the great hospitals.

On the night in question, Mr. Gladstone was
announced to speak in defence of his policy of
taxing these charities. Though it seemed an
arid topic, giving little scope to a rich imaginative eloquence like his, it was no easy matter to
secure a place in the Stranger's Gallery. Every
corner and crevice of the House were filled as
soon as the doors were open. Members, even,
were forced to resort to the galleries, so crowded
were the benches below; the ladies' gallery was
thronged with peeresses, and the leaders of London society. The world of London, at least,
knew that Mr. Gladstone was one of those rare
magicians who could make even figures eloquent.

When the orator rose from the front government bench, drew himself up, holding a small
slip of paper in his hand, and quietly looked
around on the multitude whose single gaze was
upon him, he seemed younger and more impos-
ing than he had done when standing chatting in

the lobby. You recognized at once, by his mere expression and motion, that he was already warm and proud with the ardor of forensic conflict; that he loved this arena on which he stood, and that his whole soul was in the task before him. In his first few simple sentences, one already felt the sweet and persuasive power of a voice which, even in his age, has perhaps no equal in any assembly on earth. There were the soul and life of intense earnestness in its very first tones, as the commonplace opening of the speech was uttered; now subdued, to be sure, but soon to burn out and glow with all the fire of the man's warm intellectual nature. The next thing observed was the contrast between this smooth, steady flow of words, this rising fluency of language, pouring out long and involved sentences without a pause, a hitch, an instant's loss of the right word, and the halting and hesitating oratory of most English public men. After listening to the stammering of Lord John Russell, the humming and hawing of the genial Palmerston, and the studied abruptness of Disraeli, this rapid, steady, limpid quality of Mr. Gladstone's eloquence was charming. To his wonderful fluency, the flexibility and strength as well as sweetness of his voice added striking effect; for it has depth, volume and wide range of tone, and quickly adapts itself to the rhetorical need of the moment.

His style of speaking was easy and simple. As he proceeded, he played with a piece of paper in his hand, which soon proved to contain the few notes he had prepared; and every now and then he stroked the thin hair above his forehead with his forefinger or thumb, as if to encourage the idea to come out into expression. The gestures were at first few, the clenched hand occasionally suddenly sawing the air for a moment, then falling as suddenly prone at his side. As he advanced, he often straightened himself up from a colloquial to a declamatory posture, with his head thrown back, his sunken dark eyes glistening from beneath the heavy brows, and the strong jaw seeming to set, as for a serious purpose; and then, as he passed to another branch of the subject, he would relapse into the conversational attitude again. The movements, it could be easily seen, were quite unstudied; the impulse of the moment guided the action of head or hand, or the expression of the speaking features. As he warmed to his subject, his action became more excited, and his gestures more frequent. Now, his head was almost every moment high in air, his hands would be clasped as if in appeal, he turned often to the right and to the left, or bent over the table in front of him. Every attitude was at once ungraceful and strong. The spontaneity, the earnestness, made even the orator's occasional awkwardness eloquent; while the continual, unhesitating, liquid flow of the words and sentences, and the solid chain of thought, most often diverted the listener's mind from the gestures altogether.

You recognized at once that this was not an extempore speech, in the sense of being delivered off-hand and without preparation. Every point had been thought over carefully, every series of figures conned, the array of the general current of the argument duly and methodically arranged in the mind. But the words, the sentences, the few telling figures of speech, came with voluble spontaneity. The opening deceived you somehow into the idea that the flow of the harangue would be sweet and serene throughout. But before Mr. Gladstone had been speaking fifteen minutes he seemed, as Sydney Smith said of Webster, " a steam engine in trousers." No

orator was ever more susceptible to the warm-
ing-up process, caused by the very act of speaking, than he. No orator ever became more
wrapt, more absorbed, in the task before him.
You felt profoundly that he was speaking from
the most firmly rooted convictions; that the
cause he advocated was buried deep in his heart,
and was the outcome alike of conscience and
intellectual self-persuasion. The dominant idea
with him was, not to make a great display, not
to produce a refined and polished-off bit of eloquence, but to persuade and to convince. He
produced that powerful effect upon his hearer,
which is one of the highest triumphs of oratory,
that made you feel ashamed and perverse not to
agree with him and be persuaded. I cannot
imagine even a stolid Tory squire listening to
such appeals, without feeling some dull qualm
at his own silent resistance to the persuasive
argument. There was, too, a proud consciousness of his own powers betrayed in every motion
and utterance; not vain self-conceit was this, but
the pride that assured him that these powers
might be and should be used to attain the unselfish public end he had in view. " He stands
up," as a shrewd observer once said of him, " in

the spirit of an apostle with a message to deliver, certain of its truth, and certain that *he*, and not some other man, is appointed to deliver it." That is just the impression which Mr. Gladstone has always produced, and still produces, on those who hear him speak; and this apostolic earnestness is, indeed, the chief source of his forensic power.

As an orator, Mr. Gladstone lacks the strong simplicity of Mr. Bright's Saxon English, and the wealth of illustration with which Mr. Bright illumines his subject; he also lacks the epigrammatic sparkle and subtle irony of his long-time rival, Disraeli. He has sometimes been compared to Burke, and in a few respects closely resembles the "great impeacher," in personal as well as intellectual traits. But it is doubtful whether Mr. Gladstone's speeches will be read ninety years hence, as Burke's are read now. They are too verbose. His sentences are often as well-nigh interminable as the celebrated sentences of our own secretary of state. True, the language is beautiful and forcible, the meaning clearly conveyed, and the argument pyramidal in structure and strength. But no one would put selections from Mr. Gladstone's speeches into a school reader or a book containing "Specimens of Oratory." Yet they will be eagerly read by the student of eloquence and the student of English political history. They are, for all their defects, great and noble addresses, instinct with not only the most earnest but the broadest statesmanship. They are masterly arrays of evidence, and deep reservoirs of exhaustive argument.

Mr. Gladstone's public career extends over a period of about forty-seven years. He entered the House of Commons at the age of twenty-three, in the year that the great Reform struggle ended. He may be said to have already become distinguished when he took his seat; for he had won high honors at Oxford, and the Oxford prize-men are always known and applauded throughout England. More than this, he was understood to be an ardent champion of the church, and to possess the eloquence to defend it with effect. The future Liberal leader first appeared on the political arena as what Macaulay called "a stern and unbending Tory." He owed his parliamentary seat to the favor of a great Tory magnate; and he was looked upon as the young hope of the party which then had

few "hopefuls," young or old. There was, from
the first, not the least doubt of one thing, — Mr.
Gladstone was certain to be a parliamentary success. His first speech more than justified his
reputation. It charmed and delighted everybody who heard it or read it. It suggestively
contrasted with Mr. Disraeli's break-down as a
political tyro, and the long struggle which Mr.
Disraeli made to retrieve himself and become a
power. Mr. Gladstone no sooner opened his
mouth, and let his sweet, silvery, persuasive
voice be heard, and his intense ardor and earnestness be seen, than he took high rank among
the orators of the House of Commons, and from
that time to this he has never once made what
his bitterest enemies could construe as a failure
in eloquence. He has never for a moment lost
his hold on the silence, attention, and admiration — often reluctantly awarded — of the House.
In England, oratorical success in parliament is
the almost invariable "open sesame" to political honors. Ministries need, almost above all
else, men who can speak, especially men who
can persuade. Mr. Gladstone's readiness and
fluency, and the genuineness of his eloquence,
speedily stood him in good stead. He was soon

in office; and thenceforth no ministry could be formed from the political party with whose views he at the time accorded, without providing him with a place in it. He was indispensable, first to the Tories, then to the Peelites, and finally to the Liberals; his intellectual supremacy over all his contemporaries had already been acknowledged before he had passed the limit of middle life. And this was in spite of his intellectual restlessness, and impatience of submission to party precepts and party rule. As he advanced, his opinions changed. Far from proving "a stern and unbending Tory," Mr. Gladstone was very quick to yield to new arguments, to accept new lights, to modify his views according to changing circumstances. Possessing a mind keenly sensitive to the needs of the state and of the people, he never seems to have allowed the bugbear of consistency, much less the idea of mere loyalty to a party, to stand in the way of his conversion to any cause of the justice of which he was finally satisfied. "Openness of mind," says an able English writer, "eagerness to learn, candor in the confession of past mistakes, and a readiness to admit a conscious immaturity of judgment on points which

he has not yet fully thought out," are the high
intellectual and moral qualities that belong pre-
eminently to Mr. Gladstone. So it was that the
"stern and unbending Tory" became the advanced Liberal chief who initiated the later electoral reform; that the champion of "church and
state" became the disestablisher of the Irish
church; that the ardent protectionist of 1832
became an abolisher of the corn laws in 1845;
and that the colleague of Wellington became
the colleague of Bright and the friend of Cobden
and Mill. All his life, Mr. Gladstone has been
"thinking aloud;" he has reached every stage
of his progress along the political highway,
across open plains, where his every movement
and step could be seen by a nation.

Added to these noble qualities, Mr. Gladstone
possesses others which together place him on
the highest plane of pure and moral statesmanship. It would be too much, perhaps, to say
that Mr. Gladstone has not desired office, and
is not fond of power. But if he has been thus
ambitious, there is every reason to conclude that
neither selfish greed of authority, nor a selfish
wish to be conspicuous and laden with honors,
has entered into his ambitions. Mr. Gladstone

is an indomitable toiler. He is passionately fond
of hard, long-sustained, absorbing labor. Idle-
ness for him is a misery of miseries. And he
has always been thoroughly in love with political work. He has always delighted in the perplexities of figures, in the complications of
diplomacy, and in the evolution of practical
improvement out of sentimental grievances and
moral or religious injustices. If he has desired
office and aspired to power, it was that he might
bring this intense zeal for work, this profundity
of conviction, to the service of the people. He
has again and again showed himself utterly reckless of the personal consequences to himself of
the line of reform he has bravely adopted.
Never was there a more unmanageable party
man, a more incorrigible party chief. To tem-
porize and conciliate on a great matter when
the well-being, political and social, of masses
of men and women has been at stake, have
always been abhorrent to him. If he was in
office, he was there to do a certain work; and
into it he always plunged with an ardor and a
determination which quite swept party interests
and personal perils out of sight. To make England just, as well as great and prosperous, has
been one of his most persistent aims.

The same qualities which have made Mr.
Gladstone a great statesman and reformer —
his unselfish and ardent adherence to his convictions, and his readiness to change those convictions when otherwise persuaded — have made
him one of the very worst party leaders who ever
appeared in parliament. The tact and supple-
ness, the spirit of conciliation and harmonizing,
the patience and perseverance by which the successful party chief succeeds in reconciling factions, and in bringing men of different views to
act together for the sake of party victory, seem
to have been almost utterly wanting in him. He
lacks, too, those lighter graces of leadership
which have made Mr. Disraeli so consummate
a political general. Mr. Gladstone has never
taken pains to encourage and put forward the
promising younger members of his party. He
has been very sparing of praise and encomiums
to his lieutenants. He neglects the *suaviter in
modo* which sometimes disarms the spirit of revolt in crotchety statesmen, and is too prone to
wrap himself in proud solitude in the midst of
his followers. His control over his rather bilious
and irritable temper has not always been supreme.
He has not always cared to conceal his impa-

tience and vexation at an expressed difference of opinion among his fellow Liberals; has
sometimes broken out in a grim severity of sarcasm directed against his own colleagues; and
that, too, when he was prime minister and the
leader of the House. He is not conspicuous
for those social qualities which especially tell in
politics. Always grave, always earnest and intense, Mr. Gladstone seems always to brand by
his manner any play of humor or touch of pleasant familiarity as flippant. He was never, therefore, thoroughly popular in the Liberal party in
parliament. There was no stint to the admiration of his genius which his followers felt and
betrayed; no man was ever more respectfully
looked up to; every Liberal felt his own infe-
riority to this lofty, intellectual figure. But in
this exalted admiration there evidently was but
little mixture of that personal liking, and even
affection, which Mr. Disraeli, a really colder-
hearted man, has succeeded in inspiring among
the Tories, especially among the rising talent of
Torydom. These causes served to make Mr.
Gladstone a disastrous party leader. Succeed-
ing to the command of a powerful and pretty
compact party organization, he so badly led it

that he carried it to defeat, almost to disorgani-
zation and disruption; and the comparative fee-
bleness of Liberalism to-day, when it is rather a
conglomeration of factions than a party, is due
more to Mr. Gladstone's fatal inability to lead
than to any other one circumstance.

Not only is Mr. Gladstone a bad leader; he
is, if possible, even a worse follower. Four
years ago he threw up his leadership, and the
judicious Marquis of Hartington was chosen to
succeed him. Mr. Gladstone took his place in
the rank and file. But he has proved quite
insubordinate to party discipline. More than
once he has interposed a voluntary leadership
of his own, in interference of that of Lord Hartington. Again and again he has proposed
measures and resolutions, and urged his Liberal
friends to follow him, in spite of the advice and
even entreaties of the recognized Liberal chief.
He vehemently opposed the line taken by Lord
Hartington on the subject of Ritualism, and
divided the House of Commons against him.
He as vehemently separated from Lord Hartington on the Turkish question, and proposed
and urged resolutions which created a serious
breach in the Liberal ranks. The fact is, the

commanding intellect and figure of Mr. Gladstone can never be compressed into the uniform of a party private. He *must* rule men's minds by his eloquence, his ardor, his eager enthusiasm of conscience. As long as he sits in the House of Commons, he must be a chief, subject to no other chief, with inevitable power in his voice, and dominating authority in his utterances on political policy.

We have scarcely yet glanced at Mr. Gladstone's qualities as a practical statesman; yet those qualities are, like all that pertain to him, remarkable. "In the power of giving legislative form to the policy on which the nation has determined," says an English writer, " of organizing complex and difficult details into a complete and orderly scheme, and of recommending it by inexhaustible resources of exposition and illustrations to parliament, Mr. Gladstone never had a superior, or, we may venture to say, an equal." In the intuitive recognition of what England has become in earnest in demanding, and ripe to receive, Mr. Gladstone strikingly resembles our own Lincoln. He has always kept just abreast of the people; and, sensitive to their needs and well-being and ripe desire beyond any other statesman of his time, he has also been their masterly interpreter, and their most efficient servant. Like Lincoln, quick to perceive and transfer into practical policy the popular need of the day, like Pitt he is skilful in moulding such a policy into law; but in this respect he is certainly greater than Pitt. It is rarely that noble eloquence is joined, in the same man, with a high capacity for practical work and the mastery of dry detail; yet Mr. Gladstone is the ablest financier England has produced in this century. As Chancellor of the Exchequer, his Budgets were triumphs of the financial art; not only in the rare interest he lent to figures by fascinating and illustrative statement, but in the soundness, the solidity, and the resource of the financial policy they embodied. They were exhaustive in the treatment of the money affairs of the nation, and in the fine and well-balanced adjustment of taxes and of the public expenditure. But his financial have been, perhaps, the least — certainly they are the least conspicuous — of his triumphs in practical statesmanship. It is probably true, as has been remarked of his public career, that in it, more than in that of any other man who has

lived through the same period, "the history of
England during the past forty years is reflected."
Sir Robert Peel had no more effective coadjutor
when he abolished the corn laws; Mr. Gladstone
is one of the historic group who share the honor
of having accomplished that brave and wise act.
The second reform of 1867, which was carried,
it is true, by Mr. Disraeli, was based upon the
proposals elaborated the year before by his
rival; and it may be added that Mr. Gladstone,
although in opposition, did very much to give
that reform its final practical and complete
shape. He might be well content to rest his
fame for statesmanship upon the two great acts
of his own premiership — the Irish land reform,
and the disestablishment of the Irish church.
The latter betrayed no less the supremacy of
his conscience over the impulses of his heart,
than his splendid talent for constructing a most
difficult and perplexing public measure; for he
was as ardent a churchman in 1871 as he had
been in 1835. To apply practical relief to the
grievances of Ireland was a herculean task, as
many a statesman had found to his cost before
him; but Mr. Gladstone brought to it all the
fiery zeal, the enormous capacity for work, the

ability to frame a most effective statute out
of a chaos of bewildering materials, for which
he is conspicuous far above all his contemporaries. Those two acts, the one according a large
measure of justice to Irish tenant farmers, the
other relieving Catholic Ireland of the intolera-
ble burden of an alien state church, are noble
monuments to Mr. Gladstone's political genius.

Mr. Gladstone is a many-sided man. An
orator and statesman of the first rank, he is
also a scholar, versatile in many branches of
study and research, and in some profound.
His studies of Greek literature and antiquities
are well known, for he has written works on
these subjects which would have made him
famous in the learned world, had he never sat
in parliament or wielded the destinies of the
British Empire. In "Juventus Mundi," especially, we have the fruits of an ardent and
exhaustive research into the evidences of the
historical fact of the Trojan war, which has
gone far to enlighten the controversies inspired
by the Homeric books. It is hard to tell
whether Mr. Gladstone is more in love with
classical or ecclesiastical studies; he is assuredly
deeply in love with both. His earliest essay in

letters was his book on the " Relations of Church
and State," which called forth Macaulay's famous searching but not on the whole unkindly
criticism; and to this day Mr. Gladstone has
snatched leisure from even the busiest periods
of his political career, to write essays and books
on the changing phases of ecclesiastical questions. He has always plunged with as much
enthusiasm into church debates in the House,
as into those on finance or on the Eastern problem; and within the past few years, especially,
the reviews and magazines have afforded frequent evidence of the continued vitality of his
interest in such topics, as well as the sustained
vigor of his intellectual strength.

Mr. Gladstone's writings, indeed, fully deserve
the permanent form in literature which has recently been given to them. In them are to be
perceived the same sturdy force of conviction,
the same absorbing earnestness to persuade, the
same zeal for the higher good of mankind, — and
better than all, the same lofty moral tone of
thought, which appear in his forensic productions.
He wrote one essay, at least, that was far more
than an essay; it was an historic event. This was
his series of letters on the outrageous tyranny

of the Bourbon rule in Naples. Never was there
a production more fruitful of great results; for
it is not too much to say that Mr. Gladstone's
letters to Lord Aberdeen did more to set Naples
free, and thus indirectly to give impetus to the
Italian craving for unity, than all the plots of
Mazzini or even the guerilla raids of Garibaldi.

It is always interesting to observe and note
the personal traits of a great man. Those of
Mr. Gladstone may be somewhat judged by what
has already been said of the qualities which have
been portrayed in his public capacities. Mr.
Gladstone is dead-in-earnest, even in his recreations. Consider what are the favorite pastimes
of this indomitable worker on the political field,
this knight-errant of political morals among the
nations, this hot controversialist, this one-time
ruler of the greatest of the world's empires!
Were you to visit the picturesque manor of
Hawarden, in Wales, some time during the autumn
months, you would very likely see this man of
seventy, with coat off and huge axe in hand, at-
tacking as vehemently the trunk of a giant oak,
as in the House he sometimes does what he regards as the dishonoring subterfuges of an insin-
cere cabinet. All the country round, he is

famous as the feller of big trees; and he seems to be intent on thus working off, by the most stalwart physical exercise he can find, the superfluous vitality and fire which even politics and polemics have not exhausted. And, for the time, his pleasure is just as great in subduing the stubborn oak as it was erewhile in trampling down the specious arguments of Sir Stafford Northcote, or struggling with the champions of anti-Ritualism.

The ex-premier has, however, other and serener pleasures. He is an accomplished player on the piano, which has time and again proved a soothing solace to his restless and overworked brain. His voice, the most musical voice heard within the walls of parliament, is also singularly sweet and powerful when, as he loves to do, he blends it with the harmonies of his favorite instrument. It is said that when he was prime minister he was wont, after some late and exciting debate, to return to his house in Carlton Gardens in the small hours of morning, sit down at his Erard and play a recent ballad, or perhaps an older one, suited to restore repose to his feelings of the moment. He is more fond, we are told, of sacred and ballad music, Scotch airs, and the plaintive melodies of his old friend Moore, than of the more fashionable compositions of the German masters.

In the recess, Mr. Gladstone likes to gather a circle of choice friends around him, and to visit certain congenial country houses. But those friends are almost invariably serious, intellectual men and women, rather than fashionable people; and the country houses where he is found are those of scholars, savants, and statesmen, rather than those of brilliant leaders of society. When in London, it is not very often that Mr. Gladstone is seen in the drawing-rooms where statesmen and scholars, as well as fashionables, congregate. Whether in the drawing-room or at the dinner-table, he is always the same grave, thoughtful-mannered personage that he appears in the House or on the hustings. Earnestness is not only the keynote of the man, but seems to pervade his whole life. The mere idea of Mr. Gladstone talking "small-talk" is ludicrous. Yet it would be injustice to him to leave so incomplete a picture of his character in the reader's mind. He is far from being cold-hearted or anchoritish. On the contrary, the very intense warmth and largeness of his heart glow in his eternal earnestness. He

loves the causes to which he devotes himself —
the bettering of both the moral and the social
condition of the people, the greatness of the
church, the down-trodden Italian, the long-per-
secuted Bulgarian Christian, the memory of
Homer, the rendering of justice to the Irish —
with an ardor which comes more from the large
heart than from the luminous intellect. Indeed,
Mr. Gladstone's struggle throughout his career
seems to have been to accommodate matters between his heart and his reason. His feeling and
training lead him to prefer patrician society; his
enemies have ridiculed his alleged fondness for
the companionship of dukes. The refinement,
the grace, the scholarship, the elegant manners,
the social culture of the noble caste, undoubtedly
appeal strongly to his inbred tastes. For nobility
in the abstract, too, Mr. Gladstone has an historic
and deeply rooted respect. At moments when
his indignation at the obstructive course of the
peers has been at its hottest, he has scarcely
ever been betrayed into visiting them with the
lash of his sarcasm, of which he has a supply so
abundant for adversaries in the Commons; and
there can be no doubt that his most congenial
personal associations are with the titled and an-

ciently descended ranks of society.   But the process of profound reflection extending through
long years, and strongly affected by the progress
of events and an ever-widening sphere of observation, have led him, on the other hand, to an
intellectual sympathy with the masses of the
people; and instead of consorting in political
association exclusively with the heads of historic
families, and politicians by right of birth, he at
last finds his most intimate colleagues among
the statesmen and politicians who have risen
from the middle and common classes.   The
friend of Peel and Herbert and Newcastle has
become the friend of Bright, Fawcett, and
Dilke.   Similar has been his experience in his
religious relations.   Of all men, he long stood as
the most ardent and zealous champion of the
Church of England; and to this day there is no
more enthusiastic or devout churchman.   Yet his
intellectual growth in gradual antagonism to his
feelings and impulses has been such that he, of
all men, became the chosen instrument to aim
the first indirect blow at the church establishment through its Irish sister; and signs are not
wanting that his may become the hand to strike
the axe at the trunk of the English state church

itself. Thus his reason and his conscience seem
ever to be forcing him to chastise the objects of
his love; to cut adrift from old beloved associations; to part from congenial friendships, and to
form new ties which he has not much liked to
form, but which he has felt it right to form.

And herein is to be recognized the moral
greatness of the man. The struggle between his
reason and conscience on the one hand, and the
natural impulses of his heart on the other, is the
same internal struggle in which each individual of
mankind is for ever engaged. Mr. Gladstone's
self-triumphs have ever been conspicuously brave
and heroic. The tremendous motive of ambition,
naturally apt to be so strong in an ardent-souled
young man who begins public life with a brilliant success, has never swerved him from the often
rugged and dreary path of duty. Great as he is
as an orator, as a practical statesman, as an enthusiastic student, as an untiring worker, he is
certainly greatest in his moral aspect. No
statesman in recent English political history is
so conspicuous above all others for this trait.
We read that history, and we find Pitt and Fox,
Canning and Peel, Russell and Derby — the
ablest and best of that illustrious roll — engaged

in bitter party struggles for personal supremacy. Not one of them was entirely free from yielding to the temptations, by yielding to which power came within their grasp. Mr. Gladstone's rise to power has been in spite of his moral superiority to all personal temptation. Indeed, his succession to the premiership was due, not to his own persistent seeking for it, but to his transcendent ability, and the confidence that all mankind had in the nobility of his aims. No man ever took office with a more solemn conviction that it was not a reward or delight, but a responsibility, a trust, and a burden. So pure and lofty a fame as his will surely be enduring; and its best lesson to future generations will be its moral example.

II.

BISMARCK.

THE rough and rugged majesty of Bismarck's person and bearing is a fine external typification of his mental and moral calibre. He belongs physically, as well as intellectually, to the race of the world's giants. The Brandenburgian breed of men is neither very tall nor, among other Germans, mentally superior. But the Bismarcks have been for centuries stalwart personages, stern and strong of feature and character. They have long towered among their Pomeranian countrymen; the present Bismarck has only carried upon a far vaster field the power and influence locally wielded by his ancestors for many generations. There is always a sense of disappointment and, in some sort, of astonishment, to find in a famous man of whom one has long read or heard, a diminutive person, an insignificant face. On the other hand, you are gratified to observe such a man to be as marked and superior to others in physical form and expression, as he is in the qualities that have made him great. It is not pleasant to think of poets like Pope and Scarron, warriors like Luxembourg, as pitiful and sickly humpbacks; it adds something to our estimate of men like Washington, Napoleon, Cromwell, Chatham, — and we may well add, Bismarck, — to know that their very personal appearance carried something exceptional and distinguished in it.

No one would pass Bismarck, even in a crowded assemblage of celebrities, or a court gathering of statesmen, soldiers and nobles, without pausing to look a second time. In stature he rises quite to the lofty height of his imperial master, and that master's equally tall heir apparent. His herculean shoulders seem to have been framed and knitted to bear the burdens of war and empire. His haughty, erect bearing, the chest full and solid beneath the tightly buttoned military coat, the round head, with its shining bald knob, thrown proudly back; the firm, grim mouth, set rigidly by the massive jaw; the heavy sweeping mustache, not long since tawny, but now almost snow-white; the large, round, glistening, cold, gray eyes, always full open, and made more stern by bushy, overhanging brows, indicate, as clearly

as features ever did, noble birth, patrician instincts, and self-conscious power.

It was in the great gala year of 1867, when
Napoleon III., then in the summit of his imperial
career, was entertaining the sovereigns and statesmen of Europe at the Exposition, that I first saw
Bismarck. He was then fifty-four years of age,
and he, too, seemed at that time to have reached
the full height of his renown. Interesting as it
was to see the stalwart old soldier who occupied
the throne of Prussia, the manly beauty of the
autocrat of the Russias, the grace and loveliness
of Eugenie, the secret, expressionless face of the
imperial host himself, it is doubtful whether
either of these potentates attracted the attention
which universally sought that great Pomeranian,
who already seemed a world-mover, and wore
the historic as well as the personal aspect of a
hero. The brilliant Bohemian victories of the
year before, every one knew, were of his doing
in their preparation and political plan. There
was no doubt that the vast project of an united
Germany had shaped itself quite definitely and
practically in his mind; and that his resolute
soul — the imperious and ambitious soul that he
had inherited from his mother — was determined

to bring the scheme to a not distant realization. Not a few suspected that this very Paris, now so gay and bedecked and joyous, which was fêting him as one of her choicest guests, was looked upon by him with an eye not entirely single to its beauty, and with thoughts not absolutely absorbed by admiration and gratitude. It was believed that of the two chief obstacles to German unity under the chiefship of Prussia, only one — the opposition of Austria — had been swept away; and that the next bold step of the Prussian premier would be to crush the hostility of France. Yet here he was, the guest of the sovereign whom it was doubtless in his mind sooner or later to assail, and the recipient of the bounty of the beautiful city which, three years later, he was destined to enter as a conqueror.

Bismarck showed himself freely everywhere in Paris. Each day he was to be seen riding to and fro in the imperial carriages, sometimes with the Prussian king or the emperor, sometimes quite alone. He always appeared in that commanding military costume, with glittering peaked helmet and long blue cloak, which he seems to take pride in wearing on all proper occasions. Beneath the helmet, the tawny hair, the long, sweeping, red-brown mustache, the stern eyes, the ruddy blond complexion, the strange, grim expression of the features, soon became familiar in the Paris streets. Some one has remarked his peculiar resemblance to an English bull terrier; and certainly his face has the same look of irascibleness, tenacity, and stubborn pluck which we recognize in that animal's countenance. He bore himself haughtily and silently amid the fantastic festivities of Paris. Rarely was it that a smile lighted up the iron features; seldom was he seen engaged in conversation with his companions. One could not help feeling, as he appeared sitting bolt upright in the carriage, and now and then looking down at the lively crowds with a glance of apparent contempt, that Bismarck felt uneasy at being there at all, and was half conscious that it was not quite the thing for him to be guest of a people whom the rapid tide of events was hastening to compel him to chastise. That visit to Paris, indeed, was a rather embarrassing interlude in that large political drama which he had already set upon the stage of Europe; and it was probably with a sigh of relief that he at last whirled away from Paris and from France, and returned to the Friedrichstrasse to prepare the next thrilling act.

Bismarck, as has been said, is the scion of an ancient and noble family. He was born and reared amid the luxury of ancestral acres and social rank. He was educated with all that refinement of painstaking which wealthy Germans are apt to lavish upon their children. He was a student at Göttingen, Griefswald, and Berlin. In his youth, he was called by all his comrades and neighbors, " mad Bismarck." Stalwart of frame, robust in health, his animal spirits were leonine in their roughness and exuberance; he had aggressive daring, was quick to give blow for blow, drank, revelled, and rode hard, fought duels at the university by the score, was now and then plunged into the gloomiest fits of melancholy, made love like a sentimental giant, and studied — when at all — with an absorbing energy and intentness that would have soon shattered a weaker constitution. With all these qualities, Bismarck was an aristocrat to the marrow of his bones. His pride outstripped that of his ancestors. From youth up, he was a Junker of Junkers. He inherited — and improved upon the inheritance — intense loyalty to his lord the king and to the Protestant faith, and a sublime contempt of the common people, and what they absurdly called their "rights." It is important to remember the toryism of his breeding and his nature, in order to interpret rightly the motives which have inspired his policy, and to explain the occasional apparent inconsistencies of his public career.

It is almost trite to say that Bismarck is the ablest statesman that any European country has produced during the present century. The results of his public labors have been simply colossal. He did not, of course, invent the project of German unification; it had been the dream of all the Teutonic peoples for generations. It was however, an enormous, seemingly a hopeless task. Its realization needed a hand no less firm, a soul no less courageous, a mind no less prompt and fertile in resources, an energy no less exhaustless, than Bismarck proved to possess. At the age of thirty he was a member of the Prussian Diet, and was chiefly noted for the extreme violence of his absolutist opinions. Men thought him "mad," as his college mates had done. He cut a figure in the Diet rather grotesque than otherwise. We first hear of him as violently opposing a plan of German unity; yet at that very moment nothing was so near his heart as to see

Germany one. It was because he saw that the time was not ripe; that Austria was yet too strong as a German influence; that Prussia had not grown to her full stature. Very probably at that early period, Bismarck had formed a unification plan of his own. But he was — always has been — a Prussian before he was a German. He was resolved that Germany should only become united under the leadership and sovereignty of the house of Hohenzollern. To restore the Imperial diadem to the Catholic Hapsburgs was the very last thing to which he would consent.

When, a little later, we find him acting upon the broader fields of diplomacy and the confederation, reading his course then by what we know of his subsequent policy, it is not difficult to see that the purpose to unify Germany under Prussian chiefship was already matured, and that already he had begun, by sometimes apparently reckless means, to put his mighty scheme into operation. We need not follow him step by step from his entrance upon the diplomatic stage at Frankfort to his elevation to supreme power in 1862. During that period he was vigorously battling with the pretensions of Austria, observing narrowly the temper of the French emperor and court, and gathering about him a group of adherents and instruments who were to be of use to him in the not distant future. Meanwhile, he had won the confidence of the king, and impressed the evidence of his genius upon the minds of the German people.

Called, in 1862, to the presidency of the Prussian cabinet, Bismarck for the first time found full scope and elbow-room in which to pursue his almost insuperable design. And now for the first time he displayed those marked qualities and characteristics, which have since become so familiar to men. Bluntly and brutally frank; contemning the tortuous and mysterious methods of diplomacy which had become traditional in Europe; imperious alike towards colleagues and towards opponents; plain, pithy, and strong in speech; indefatigable in labor; assuming the whole burden of administration; defiant of opposition; rude, rough, and little scrupulous in means; arbitrary and irascible of temperament; iron-willed, riding rough-shod over everybody and everything in his way, — it is no wonder that during the first year or two of his premiership, Bismarck was by all odds the best-hated man in

Prussia. Diet after Diet was chosen to oppose him, and only went to Berlin to vote down every proposal he brought before them. But to this Junker noble, the constitution that had been granted was an evil, possibly a blunder. He was apparently as indifferent to popular opposition as to Austrian intrigues. He was sublimely contemptuous of the representatives of the people. When, therefore, they voted down his schemes, he simply resorted to methods as natural to a man of his bringing-up and temperament as anything in the world. He truculently told them he could do without them, and sent them about their business. He was bound to rule and to carry out his great project, constitution or no constitution, people or no people. Every Diet that opposed him was incontinently packed off home. He thus virtually had the whole field to himself; with his large personality he occupied it, and held it against all comers, even against the Prussian people. Popular rights were nothing to him; what were they to this herculean despot, compared with the realization of that glorious dream of national unity which had long been dreamed by the most illustrious German statesmen and poets? Nor was German unity the only lofty prize at which he was grasping. To make Germany supreme in Europe, as well as a unit in herself, was the purpose of his daring ambition; to make William of Prussia a greater potentate than Napoleon of France or Alexander of the Russias, was the object he set before him; and every obstacle in the way of this, be it a Diet, a people, or three or four foreign nations, he was grimly resolved to crush.

See with what consummate adroitness and stern courage he advanced to the consummation of his purpose; on how vast a scale his design was developed; what a far and mighty reach his mind, long foreseeing and toweringly ambitious, took! That design was scarcely less gigantic than was that of Napoleon himself; and there was this difference between Napoleon and Bismarck, that the latter *succeeded.* His idea was a loftier one than mere personal glory and advancement; loftier even than the aggrandizement of a nation; it was the unification of a race. The first step was to avail himself of the opportunity, afforded by the death of the King of Denmark, to detach Schleswig and Holstein from the Scandinavian kingdom. This Bismarck did with the aid of Austria, meaning at that very time to filch

from Austria every fruit of the joint victory. It
is needless to point out with what success this
first move in the mighty game was played.
Then the time was ripe to depose Austria from
her predominance in the Germanic confederation,
and to put Prussia in her place. Not only the
political plan, but a considerable part of the military plan of the memorably short, sharp, and
decisive campaign of 1866, was conceived in
Bismarck's brain; a fortnight's action, and a
single great battle, drove Austria from all federal
connection with her sister German states, and
so crippled her as to satisfy Bismarck that he
would not henceforth have her hostility to reckon
with. The mightiest and most uncertain struggle was still to come. There is no doubt that,
from the moment Sadowa had been won, Bismarck and Von Moltke directed their thoughts
to the inevitable conflict with France. Napoleon,
indeed, had proclaimed aloud the doctrine of
nationalities. But the Prussian statesman well
knew that Napoleon would not, without resistance, permit the application of that doctrine to
Germany. The smaller German dynasties —
Hanover, Würtemberg, Bavaria, Saxony, Nas-
sau — lay prone at the feet of the Hohenzol-

lerns; but so long as a hostile nation frowned from the banks of the Rhine, they might still hope to be released from their new and galling bondage.

If the war of 1870 appeared to the superficial looker-on as recklessly provoked and forced on by France, it is one more testimony to the masterly adroitness of Bismarck. He succeeded in luring France into war at the moment when Germany was prepared for the encounter, and France was not; and not only that, but in casting upon France the onus and odium of being the first to disturb the peace of the world. We now know that the plan of the campaign of 1870 lay in Von Moltke's pigeon-holes in 1866; and that at least three years before it opened, Bismarck had predicted it almost to the very month, and had clearly foreshadowed its political as well as its military results. The candidature of a Hohenzollern to the Spanish throne, the insult to Benedetti, were dramatic situations prepared deliberately in the Friedrichstrasse at Berlin. Bismarck knew only too well Napoleon and the French. He had served to good purpose as an ambassadorial spy at the court of the Tuileries: he probably knew the inner tone and feeling of Napoleon's counsels, and the temper of the French people quite as well as Ollivier and Gramont. He chose his time; his plans were ripe. He counted beforehand on what took place; every move in the game was foreordained. No statesman ever achieved a more magnificent triumph than that which Bismarck enjoyed when, on the 17th of January, 1871, he stood in the stately hall at Versailles, panoplied in his military gear, and listened to the proffer by Bavaria, Saxony, and Würtemberg, of the imperial diadem to William of Prussia. There were no longer formidable enemies to fear. The two colossi who had barred the way were prostrate in the dust. The German states had become reconciled by the pitiless logic of force to Prussian ascendency; and the stupendous plot conceived at least nine years before had been brought to at least material fruition.

It might be thought that such a result would have sated the ambition of any public man. Had Bismarck retired to the always-welcome repose of Varzin, to his much-loved family, his horses, dogs and fruitful fields, after returning from France, and left to others the imminent task of imperial reconstruction, he would have left a renown more illustrious than that of any statesman of the century. But his iron energies

seemed to derive new strength from military success. He bent himself to the drier duties of statecraft with the same keen and tireless vigor which
had already accomplished so much. If he had
lesser obstacles to encounter, they were nevertheless perplexing and harassing. It is easier to
pull down than build up, as is testified by the fate
of the Ephesian dome. To compel the complete
reconciliation of dynasties stripped of pomp and
power, and of peoples jealous and distrustful of
Prussian rule, to carry out a plan which should
at once secure German unification and Prussian
predominance, to grapple with the intrusive
authority of the Pope and subordinate an hitherto almost independent church to the control of
the state; these were the labors immediately
before the chancellor, and pressing upon him.
But these were not all. There was that other
ambition, already partly fulfilled, but still not
permanently achieved; the ambition to set Germany above the nations, to make her the arbiter
of Europe, to institute her the guide, director,
and pioneer of the march of European events;
to hold the deciding voice in the areopagus of
the world. Bismarck was as sternly bent on this,
it would seem, as upon German unity itself.

The period which has elapsed since the treaty
of Versailles has developed in a clear light Bismarck's qualities as a statesman dealing with
home affairs, and as a party leader. He has,
indeed, been a party leader in but one sense.
He has never been the recognized and consist-
ent chief of either of the great parties which
divide German opinion; he has only led those
combined sections of parties which have come
together from time to time to support his policy.
It has been said that Bismarck is a patrician by
birth, breeding, and conviction settled upon experience. The idea of making a free as well as
a united Germany seems rarely to have occurred
to him; and only on such occasions as it advanced some ulterior end he had in view, has
he appeared to lean to the liberal side. His
part has been to attain military and national
glory and power. When was Bismarck ever
known to become warm in the advocacy of
oppressed peoples; unless, indeed, to champion the cause of oppressed peoples was to reach
some end entirely apart from their liberation?
For the well-nigh obsolete Prussian constitution
he has never pretended to cherish any exalted
respect. He has not hesitated to violate it with

cynical frankness and autocratic disdain whenever it served his purpose. His rule, indeed,
from first to last, has been that of an autocrat.
He has absorbed the royal power into his own.
The old emperor has never ventured to resist
him, not even when Bismarck, quite recently,
dictated the loosening of the close and affectionate ties which, owing in a large degree to
the near relationship of the sovereigns, have
for years bound Germany with Russia. It is
well known that within the circle of the German
court Bismarck has enemies who would be formidable against any other man on earth. It
seems to matter little to him, however, that the
empress and the crown prince have long desired
to strip him of his authority. He apparently
rises from each assault of opposition, whether
from the palace or in the Reichstag, endowed
with a fresh and more obstinate strength. Patrician and autocrat as he is to the marrow of his
bones, however, Bismarck has been forced sometimes into strange party alliances. Cynically
unscrupulous in his methods, he has espoused
causes in which he had no heart, and has joined
with men with whom he had no real sympathy,
in order to reach some far-seen goal, of which

his whilom political bed-fellows had no glimpse.
When the aristocratic Junkers, narrower of vision
than himself, feared lest Germany should swallow
Prussia, instead of Prussia Germany, and so opposed his schemes, he made truce with the liberals and led them from victory to victory. He
waged successful war on the Catholic hierarchy;
he granted some minor reforms; he accepted
colleagues like Falk, and even dallied with so-
cialists like Hasselmann. When, in the great
work of German unification, he found it unne-
cessary or impossible any longer to wear the
mask of reform, he stood not on the order of
his desertion of his liberal allies, but deserted
them abruptly, and sought and easily won the
support of the Junkers and the Catholics.

It is interesting to observe Bismarck as, in the
legislative palace at Berlin, he sits on the central
bench of the Reichstag, which is set apart for
the imperial ministers. He usually enters just
before the house is called to order, and with a
haughty nod here and there, sits plump down
into his chair, apparently unconscious of the multitude of eyes that are fixed upon him. He begins
at once his work of signing papers, glancing
rapidly over despatches, and giving orders to

the secretaries who stand by. Now and then
he throws a quick glance across the chamber;
then settles down again, folds his arms across
his breast, and seems to be carrying on a double
process of listening to what is said, and of meanwhile thinking hard. But if Herr Lasker or
Herr Haenel happens to be delivering an eloquent tirade against the government, you can
easily read upon the chancellor's grim face, and
in his nervous, petulant movements, the emotion
which is agitating him. He is not one of those
nerveless men who can listen with a stolid face
and contemptuously placid smile to the invec-
tives of his antagonists. Irritable, imperious,
yet thin-skinned and sensitive, Bismarck never
seems to care to conceal the annoyance or anger
so easily aroused in his breast by opposition.
At such a time you will see him contract his
bushy brows, look rapidly around the chamber
as if to take stock of his enemies, and finally
rise to his feet amid a sudden hush and breathless attention. In a delivery broken, abrupt,
spasmodic, with a voice husky and apparently
always finding its breath with difficulty, — except at certain moments of high passion, when
it rings out strong, clear and defiant, — with his

big hands clutching the shining buttons of his
military tunic, or savagely twirling and twisting
a paper or a pencil, he proceeds to reply to the
attack. His round gray eyes flash brightly and
fiercely, his large frame sways to and fro, his
face grows red, his legs are sometimes crossed,
then suddenly drawn wide apart; and he goes
on in the simplest, clearest, frankest language,
to justify his acts and repel the assertions of his
antagonist. Every one is astonished at his frankness; his blunt avowal of his motives; his unequivocal declarations of future policy; his
merciless handling, not only of his immediate
opponent, but of all his opponents, and of men
and courts outside of Germany. It is a part of
his adroitness to seem imprudently frank; his
apparent imprudence and recklessness are, we
may be sure, calculated beforehand. But there
can be no doubt that his wrath is genuine; or
that the greatest difficulty he encounters in debate is that of keeping in check his most unruly
temper.

When we follow Bismarck from the chancel-
lerie and the Reichstag, from the palace and the
council chamber, to his homes in the Friedrichstrasse and at Varzin, he appears to us under

many fresh and more pleasing aspects. For
this grim, iron-souled chief, whose courage, will,
determination, and despotic temper are so irresistible on the public arena, is really one of
the most human of men. He is still, though
often oppressed by well-nigh insufferable neural-
gic pains, as fond of a frolic as a boy. He is
far happiest in his home, surrounded by a family
than which there never was a family more ten-
derly and chivalrously beloved. He has a great,
affectionate, generous heart; his ardent devotion
to those who have won his love is in the mouths
of all Germany. His home, too, is a temple, in
which the household gods are many. In speaking of his quiet, domestic, sweet-tempered wife,
he once said, " She it is who has made me what
I am." At one of the most brilliant periods of
his life he wrote to this congenial partner: "I
long for the moment when, established in our
winter quarters, we sit once more around the
cheerful tea-table, let the Neva be frozen as
thick as it will." These winter quarters were
the massive, three-story house, No. 76 Friedrichstrasse, the chancellor's official residence.
A sentry's box at the front gate indicates its
public nature; within, liveried attendants mov-

ing to and fro betray that this great man, simple
and robust as are his tastes, must still maintain
some show of state. The broad stairway is
adorned by two stone sphinxes, which seem to
symbolize Bismarck's policy, if not his character.
Beyond, are the larger apartments of the house,
— the drawing and reception rooms; while still
more remote, and only accessible to those especially honored by Bismarck's friendship, is the
large, plain, curiously furnished library, where
he at once performs the burden of his labors
and takes his chief comfort. The windows of
the library overlook an umbrageous park; the
room itself is garnished with suits of armor, box-
ing gloves, foils, swords, and other paraphernalia
of war and the " manly arts." Time was when
Bismarck used to sit there, drinking big draughts
of mixed porter and champagne, smoking a
bottomless student pipe, and working like a
giant, till far into the earlier hours of the morning. Latterly, tortured by neuralgia, he has given
up these midnight indulgences and labors, and
sits with his family in the common sitting-room.

It is not here in the Friedrichstrasse, however,
amid the bustle of the crowded city and swarms
of officials and satellites, that Bismarck takes his

chief delight. It is only at Varzin, near by his ancestral home, among the scenes of his mad and rollicking youth, that he most fully enjoys the luxury of living. When away, he is constantly longing for Varzin. He once said: " I often dream that I see Varzin — all the trees that I know so well, and the blue sky; and I fancy that I am enjoying it all."

Ample acres, and all the appurtenances of a prosperous and well-kept landed estate surround the spacious Pomeranian mansion of the chancellor. The stables shelter many thoroughbreds, the kennels are crowded with Bismarck's favorite dogs. The conservatories teem with rare fruits and flowers; and in all these things the master takes a keen and watchful interest. But he is most often found at Varzin, as at Berlin, in his study. This is a six-sided apartment, furnished with rugged simplicity. An enormous chimney and open fireplace fill in one of the corners; on either side of which rises a column bearing a coat-of-arms on an emblazoned shield. Bismarck is proud of his blood and his ancestry. After the French war, he added to his coat-of-arms the banners of Alsace and Lorraine, and chose as his motto, " Trinitate Robur," — " My strength in trinity,"—an old family device. "And," suggested a friend, "it may also signify 'my strength in the three-in-one God.'" "Quite so," replied the prince, gravely. "That was what I meant." A bust of the emperor surmounts the chimney; while before it are placed two stiff, high-backed chairs. The walls are adorned, as Bismarck everywhere is fond of adorning them, with many curiosities; there are Tunisian sabres and Japanese swords, Russian hunting knives and braces of pistols, military caps and quaint bits of armor. The furniture of the room comprises sofas, divans, and the chancellor's writing-desk covered with green cloth, and having upon it a white porcelain inkstand and a two armed student lamp; on a small table at one side is a large Bible, evidently much used; everything is solid, plain and substantial, like Bismarck himself. This feature of simple comfort is discernible, indeed, throughout the house. Nor is it without its mysterious staircase. Such a one leads from a corridor into unknown regions. "The castle keep?" once asked a friend, pointing to the door. "That is my sally-port," said Bismarck; and he went on to explain that it led to a path

in the woods, whither the great man was fain
incontinently to retreat when threatened by a
raid of unwelcome guests.

Many of Bismarck's most attractive personal
traits are hinted to us by his surroundings.
Once within the serene atmosphere of Varzin,
the stern chancellor becomes the devoted family
man, the enthusiastic sportsman, the frank and
talkative friend, and even the genial wit. Those
who have been privileged to hear his conversation, declare it to be replete with brilliant sallies,
humorous hits, and graphic descriptions. At
his ease he is one of the frankest, most genial,
most entertaining of men. Adamant as he
seems in public, he has been known to feel so
bitterly the stings of hostile sarcasm and criticism as to give way to fits of weeping. When,
during the Austrian war, the German generals
desired to push on and invade Hungary, Bismarck strenuously opposed the project; but his
arguments were vain. Chagrined at his failure
to convince them, he suddenly left the room,
went into the next, threw himself upon the bed,
and wept and groaned aloud. "After a while,"
he says, "there was silence in the other room,
and then the plan was abandoned." His tears
had conquered where his arguments had failed.

His mode of life is peculiar. Being often sleepless, his usual hour of rising is ten in the morning. His breakfast is simple, consisting generally of a cup of tea, two eggs, and a piece of bread. At dinner he eats and drinks, like a true Pomeranian, copiously and freely. His princely appetite, indeed, is described as being truly voracious. His table groans with a super-abundance of rich and indigestible food, and dizzy concoctions of champagne and porter, sherry and tea. " The German people," said he on one occasion, alluding to the many hampers of his known favorite meats, fish, and fruits sent him from all quarters, " are resolved to have a fat chancellor."

Sometimes, like lesser folks, Bismarck has fits of the blues and of brooding ; which can scarcely be wondered at when we consider his self-indulgence at table. On these occasions he distresses those around him by the most forlorn reflections. Once he declared that he had made nobody happy by his public acts — neither himself, nor his family, nor the country. " I have had," he went on gloomily, " little or no pleasure out of all I have done — on the contrary, much annoyance, care and trouble." In brighter moods he takes all this back, and revels, with almost boyish exultation, in the splendor of his state strokes, and the new face he has put upon the world's events.

"Where is my dog?" was Bismarck's first exclamation when, on a recent visit to Vienna, he alighted from the railway train. Never did a man cherish a fonder affection for the brute creation than this king-maker and world-mover. He watched by the side of his dying "Sultan" as he might have done over a favorite child, and begged to be left alone with him in the final hour. When the faithful old friend gasped his last breath, Bismarck, with tears in his eyes, turned to his son and said: "Our German fore-fathers had a kind belief that, after death, they would meet again, in the celestial hunting-grounds, all the good dogs that had been their faithful companions in life. I wish I could be-lieve that!" For children Bismarck has an ardent fondness. His bright little grand-chil-dren are the very joy of his old age. On every occasion, he seems to take delight in humoring and pleasing the young. Curiously commingled in his large nature are sentiment and satire, kind-liness and humor. One day he was taking a

walk with his wife at the famous watering-place
of Kissingen. As they were about to turn down
a side path, the chancellor saw just beyond a
rustic family, evidently anxious to catch a good
glimpse of him. The youngest daughter, a girl
of ten, started forward, and with an expression
half-timid, half-bold, approached, staring at him.
Bismarck at once turned aside and sat down on
a rustic bench by the road, until the girl had
passed; when rising, he bowed his most stately
bow to her, said gravely, "Good morning, miss,"
and proceeded down the secluded path.

There can be no doubt of Bismarck's sturdy
personal courage. One striking incident in his
career has proved that to all time. One day in
1866, as he was returning home from the palace
through the Under den Linden, he was shot from
behind by an assassin. He turned short, seized
the miscreant, and though feeling himself
wounded, held the man with iron grasp until
some soldiers came up. He then walked rapidly
home, sat down with his family and ate a hearty
dinner. After the meal was over, he walked up
to his wife and said, "You see, I am quite well; "
adding, "you must not be anxious, my child.
Somebody has fired at me; but it is nothing, as

you see." It was the first intimation she had had of the attempted tragedy.

These necessarily rapid glances at Bismarck's career and character may fitly be brought to a close by referring to the depth and sincerity of his religious faith and feelings. In an age when scepticism and atheism are especially rampant among his countrymen, Bismarck adheres stoutly to the sturdy creed of his fathers. "I do not understand," he once wrote to his wife, "how a man who thinks about himself, and yet knows and wishes to know nothing of God, can support his existence, out of very weariness and disgust. I do not know how I bore it formerly. If I were now to live without God as then, I would not know in very truth why I should not put away life like a soiled robe."

This simple fervor of humble and deep-rooted faith seems to me to shed greater lustre on his full, troubled, but triumphant life, than the conquest of Austrian or Frank, the rebuilding of a fallen empire, the sway of a power which bends all Europe to its will, or even that lofty mastery over event and circumstance which must record his name the highest on the illustrious roll of the statesmen of our century.

III.

GAMBETTA.

IMAGINE a figure of medium height, but ungainly, awkward, heavy, somewhat obese, and loose-jointed; the limbs short, large, and far from firmly knit; the head joined to rounded shoulders by a short thick neck suggestive of a tendency to apoplexy; the shoulders not only rounded, but high and heavy; the head larger below than above, broad near the neck and at the jaws, narrow and rather flat at the top; wanting in veneration, as the phrenologists would tell us, but great in passion, in combativeness, and in language; a fine, well-set forehead, however, wide just above the eyes, and slightly sloping to the hair; a still finer intellectual brow, the best feature but one of the countenance — that one being an exceedingly well-cut, expressive, handsome, full-lipped mouth, but half concealed beneath mustache and beard; one eye apparently permanently closed, the other small, black, at times piercing and

wide-open, but usually half-closed, like the
eye of a near-sighted man who brings his
lids together the better to discern some object,
or like a shrewd person who would let you
know, by "the expression of his eye," that
he knows more than he tells; a large, thick,
unsensitive nose, bold and Jewish, with small
nostrils; the attractive mouth shaded by a
heavy, jet black mustache, which joins on
either side a beard also mostly jet black, with
a slight tinge of gray; the hair fine, straight,
once black, but nearly gray now just where
it is smoothly brushed back from the temples
over the large ears, and falling in a curve behind over the neck: the complexion of an un-
healthy, bilious hue of pale yellow; the face
indolent in general expression, giving scarcely
the slightest hint of unusual ability of any sort,
and the movement slouchy and careless, non-
chalant and often heavy, as if the man were
weary of carrying his superabundance of flesh.

This man, too, is evidently uneasy at being
well-dressed. He is manifestly uncomfortable in
the broadcloth and white necktie which the eti-
quette of his high office has forced upon him.
The broadcloth does not fit, the white necktie

is clumsily tied, and is usually awry. He cannot
help an old Bohemian habit of his, of hanging
his fat hands lazily in his trousers' pockets,
whither they are always wandering, even when
the moment requires an attitude of dignity.
Observe him as he saunters through the fres-
coed corridors of Versailles, talking, perhaps,
with half a dozen of his colleagues as he goes.
He says little; the others talk and he nods, and
now and then utters, in a deep, sonorous voice,
a sentence to which the others pay respectful
heed. His hands are hanging in his pockets;
the little white flower in his button-hole is crum-
pled; he almost seems out of place among these
elegantly attired, trim-whiskered, elegant-man-
nered men, the legislators of France. Yet there
is no duke or statesman among them to whom,
as he passes among the ever-increasing group of
deputies, so much deference is paid as to this
rather uncouth and not at first sight at all prepossessing personage.

He enters the old Versailles theatre, on whose
boards Molière once jibed and gambolled, and
where the magnificent monarch used to lounge
amid his gorgeous court; now the hall of the
deputies of republican France. He passes

slowly among the benches of the Left. There
he is at once surrounded by a large, admiring
group. The talk is of the important events or
measures of the day. This man is the centre of
attraction, the unquestioned oracle of the group.
And now he rouses himself. He is no longer
the listless fat man of the corridor. His voice
rolls out loud, full, deep, in tones as warm and
as musical as ever man heard. He gesticulates
— every gesture is force, vigor, eloquence. He
talks with a warm inspiration, in an authorita-
tive manner, quite conscious of his mastery over
his companions, and utters ideas which none
dispute, or more than demur at.

There was a time — a year or two ago —
when he would have taken a seat in the midst of
the deputies of the Left; and would have sat,
when the president rang his bell to call the
Chamber to order, in a slouching attitude, now
and then turning right or left to say something
to a neighbor, and listening intently to what
went forward. Then, when a scene of excite-
ment occurred — as it often did and does in that
Chamber — when deputies were drowning the
voice of the speaker in the tribune, and shaking
their fists in each other's faces, and hurrying

down to confront each other with hostile gesture and menace of tongue and attitude in the open space below the benches — on such an occasion you might have seen him rise, raise his arm, extend his hand, and by the powerful persuasion of his voice and manner quell the tumultuous mood of his hot-headed followers. Then, too, amid a stillness as deep as that of a mountain solitude, you might have seen him at a certain moment leap from his seat, thrust back his straggling locks, and with long stride and head aloft advance to and ascend the tribune; whence would thereupon flow the richest and most resistless eloquence that a French assemblage has heard, since, in the same Versailles, Gabriel Riquetti de Mirabeau shook throne and caste with the sudden thunder of his wordy onslaught.

But now the personage we have described ascends, not the tribune, but the presidential platform, and promptly at the designated hour rings his bell and summons deliberation out of the babel of voices. The dignity in which he seemed so lacking a little while ago, now sits as easily upon him as did his indolence; while the strong grasp with which he once held his partisans, now holds the entire assembly. He is their

master, and readily and vigorously maintains
his mastery. An intense and impetuous partisan, he shows himself capable of a Roman im-
partiality. The sharp stroke of reprimand, the
quick check of parliamentary order, fall upon
republican and monarchist alike. The power
of the chair is sustained intact. His presence of
mind is never once suspended. The despatch of
business under his rule is marvellously rapid.
He holds the reins of this turbulent, excitable,
sometimes riotous body, with the hand and
nerve of a Titan; every deputy feels the bit jerk
in his mouth at the slightest rebellion. Every
man feels that there resides in the chair a
power within a power; the power of individual
strength and command supplementing the power
endowed by the rules, by the representation of
law, and typified by the mace. A more un-
promising presiding officer than this man would
have seemed to be a year ago, could not be
conceived. An awkward, heavy person, a man
easily aroused to white-hot passion, who often
broke through all self-restraint and violated
every rule he is now called on to enforce, whose
whole being seemed wrapped in the design to
crush out one of the great parties in the nation,

one who could not be supposed, considering his unstudious and careless habits, to have deeply conned parliamentary procedure, seemed to be the last person capable of filling well the *fauteuil* of M. Grévy and M. Buffet. Yet he has proved a far more able president than either.

Sometimes men leap from obscurity to fame in a day. One of this rare sort is Leon Gambetta. It would, perhaps, be too much to say that his sudden rise was the result of accident; for had he not been a man of genius, the opportunity would have been offered him in vain. But the opportunity to show men what there was in him was accidental. On a certain day in 1868, Jules Favre, the renowned advocate, statesman, and academician, had a great cause to plead; a cause, however, more political than legal. But that day he was ill; some one must take his place; and, at a somewhat rash venture, he chose as his substitute an almost absolutely unknown, out-at-elbows, loud-talking Bohemian café-orator. M. Favre knew Gambetta but little; and mainly knew him as an ardent and outspoken republican. The mere issue of the trial, which was that of certain editors for opening their columns to the Baudin subscription, was nothing. At a time when, under the empire, free speech was forbidden the republicans on the platform, such trials were seized upon by republican orators as the occasions of fierce attacks upon the Napoleonic régime. What was needed, then, was a bold, eloquent, devil-me-care, red-hot republican, who would stand up and lash the empire without mercy, before a bench of imperial judges.

Gambetta electrified all France by his speech. It was a tremendous indictment against Napoleonism. Never did an orator produce a more immediate or more overwhelming effect. When Gambetta lay down that night his name was ringing in every club and on every boulevard in Paris.

The broad road of political fortune lay open before him. The next day he was a recognized leader among the republicans. His audience had long been the seedy loungers of the Café Procope. It now included all France, and there were many listeners outside of France. Yesterday an impecunious Bohemian, living in a garret, shabby of dress, and often short in the matter of food; to-day a deputy-elect of the city of Marseilles (as the successor of Berryer), taking counsel with and listened to by the " silver-grays" of the republican party; very soon the man in the Chamber who, of all others, was most dreaded and hated by Rouher and his intolerant imperialist majority. For now Gambetta talked as no other man talked. He spoke more boldly, what was worse, far more eloquently, than the boldest and most eloquent sages of the days of '48.

Nowhere is the curiosity about the antecedents of a man who has become notorious strained to a higher pitch than in gossiping Paris. People began to ask who this oratorical athlete was, and whence he came; and on inquiry learned that he was the son of an Italian grocer at Cahors, in midland France, "of poor but respectable parents," descended from grocers on one side, and chemists on the other; of warm Genoese blood; destined, at first, to be a priest, as were Renan, Victor Hugo, and Rochefort before him; expelled, however, from the priest-making seminary to which he had been sent, with the message to his father from the superior, "You will never make a priest of him, he has an utterly undisciplinable character;" resolved now to be a lawyer and a politician. It was told how that, one day, he was playing in a carpenter's shop, when one of his companions, in sport, made a lunge at him with a pointed stick, which thrust the right eye out of its socket; and so his disfigurement, apparent to all men, was explained to the world.

Gambetta, as a republican chief in the ominous days of 1868–70, carried with him into the arena all his old audacity, big-voiced loudness, Bohemian indifference to dress and manners, and absolute ignorance of what fear is. As he appeared in those days in the Chamber, according to one who then saw him, " He disdained all the classic attitudes of rhetoric, flung his arms about him, banged his fist down upon the first thing that came uppermost, — book, hat, or desk, — rang his voice through the wildest changes from the roar to the falsetto, and would have seemed to a deaf man the maddest contortionist at large. But if you listened to him, you were not likely to forget it. His oratory had all the defiance, energy, and fire of youth in it. He never hesitated for a word, spoke headlong, every one of his phrases being colored with that picturesque imagery of the south, always vivid, always new, and soaring at times to surprising heights in beauty of sentiment."

It was when thus roused to a great and noble oratorical effort, in the face of an irresistible and submissive imperialist majority, and defiant of the prevailing influences around him, that the writer first saw the future dictator, on the floor of the Chamber in the Palais Bourbon. The contrast between his heavy, uncouth figure, his slouching manner, his shabby dress, his rather repelling *tout ensemble*, and the appearance and bearing of the group of republican deputies around him, was the first impression conveyed to the mind. There were the venerable and prim-looking Garnier-Pagés; the leonine Jules Favre, his thick locks feathering high above his forehead; the portly Jules Simon, as stately and sedate as a count of the old régime; and Eugene Pelletan, with dark flashing eye, and delicate refinement of feature, the *beau idéal* of a cultured Frenchman of letters. How little they seemed to have in common with this big, loud, burly, rough, ill-dressed fellow, who appeared as an intruder among them! Yet, in another five minutes, when his deep, full voice rang out, or sank to sweetest and gentlest accents; when he held a hostile chamber absolutely spell-bound and silent with the matchless magic of his elo-

quence; how he was transfigured, how you for-
got the shabby coat, the Bohemian slouch, —
how *now* he towered above every one of the
historic figures around him!

He became, indeed, terrible to the empire.
He boldly told Ollivier, the "reform" premier,
from the tribune, that the "irreconcilables" only
accepted Ollivier's concessions as "a bridge to
the republic." As events drew near to the
supreme catastrophe after Sedan, Gambetta
foresaw what was coming, and felt that his opportunity for dealing a fell blow at Napoleonism
was near. But now he was walking amid mysterious dangers. Shortly after the first defeats of
the French in 1870, and after Paris had been
put in a state of siege, an attempt was made by
the Palikao ministry to kidnap the popular tribune. "All my footsteps are dogged," said Gambetta to a friend; "and my poor aunt advises
me to carry a revolver. But that would do no
good." Before he could be got rid of, however,
Sedan was fought and lost. Gambetta saw that
the time for action had come. The Chamber,
next day, was crowded. No sooner had it been
called to order than Jules Favre rose and moved
the deposition of the Napoleon dynasty. The

motion was, passed with but feeble opposition. Then Gambetta rose with one hand grasping the lapel of his coat, the other raised high above his head, and in a stentorian voice that, it is said, was clearly heard by the crowd in the courtyard outside, moved that the republic be declared established. Again the assembly yielded assent to the demand of the republican chiefs. The next thing was to form a provisional government; nor from this could Gambetta be left out. Its three principal members were Gambetta, Jules Favre, and General Trochu. It had not been in existence a fortnight before Gambetta was confessedly its ruling spirit; a month had not elapsed before he was *the* provisional government, its other members being virtually his clerks and messengers.

At thirty-two years of age, then, the son of the grocer of Cahors was the absolute dictator of France. It is often asked what opportunity Shakspeare could have had to acquire the legal and medical knowledge displayed in his dramas. It is no less a puzzle, perhaps, where and when Leon Gambetta learned the arts of government and war. His wonderful mastery of men, his tremendous will, his genius for persuasion, the ceaseless activity of his brain, the immense vigor of his action, the rapidity of his perceptions, were perhaps innate; but where did he pick up the vast knowledge of detail in two of the most difficult of human sciences, which he displayed during that troublous and terrible time when he held, undisputed, the reins of absolute power? Yet see what he did in that gloomy period. He himself organized the only army — the army of the Loire — which even temporarily checked the flood of German invasion; the only army which won a victory. The chaos in the civil administration of France, brought about by the collapse of the empire and the unparalleled disasters which had fallen on the country, Gambetta transformed into order. Riot and insurrection in the hot-beds of fanaticism were repressed by his strong hand. He raised money to equip troops, and send them to the front. He created generals, prefects, mayors. He presided over the councils of the central authority, and himself carried into prompt effect the decisions of those councils. The wonder is, as we read of the immense amount of work he went through from day to day, when he could have eaten or slept. Practically and actually he was at once the chief magistrate and the commander-in-chief. If he failed to rehabilitate France, to expel the German hordes from her soil, to protect Paris from the desecrating presence of the foe, it was because no amount of genius could have achieved these results. But he proved himself a statesman of the very first order. His talent for organization was shown to be as marvellous as the power of his eloquence and the strength of his individuality.

Nor is there evidence wanting of Gambetta's fervent patriotism. What an opportunity this warm-blooded, ambitious young man of thirty-two had to imitate the *rôle* of a Napoleon! All the powers of the state in his hands; the generals and the prefects men of his own choice; the country, rent by its misfortunes, seeming to need a master spirit; his colleagues submissive to his Titanic will; opposition disarmed and powerless. He had not even the perils of an Eighteenth Brumaire or a Second of December to fear. To seize upon supreme power, and to use it to make his dictatorship not only supreme, but permanent, was apparently easy. Yet no thought of such treachery seems to have entered his head. Just as soon as he could he appealed

to France to elect an Assembly to make peace
with the Germans. He knew well that this Assembly would take to itself the vast executive
powers he now wielded. He knew that the
representatives of France must be, for a time,
its supreme governors. He himself must step
down from the exalted height to which circumstances and his own genius had raised him. But
he did not delay a day in summoning this power,
that must supersede his own, into existence; and
when the National Assembly met at Bordeaux,
he laid his authority at its feet as quietly and
submissively as if no passion of ambition had
ever stirred his breast.

His almost superhuman toil during those
stormy months had impaired a constitution
never very robust; and now the reaction came.
Throughout the negotiations for peace, the formation of the government of the "National Defence," the rise and bloody suppression of the
commune, Gambetta lived in enforced retire-
ment. His spirit was amid those exciting scenes,
but his state of health warned him to keep aloof
from them. It was not until the administration
of Thiers had succeeded alike in making peace
with the victorious Germans, and in establishing

itself as the executive authority in France, that the ex-dictator again reappeared upon the scene. His entrance as a deputy into the Assembly was so quiet that it might be said to have been almost unnoticed. Indeed, at that moment he was unpopular. The rashness and unavailing boldness of his defence of the territory were sharply criticised on almost every hand. Thiers, in a moment of vehement passion, called him "a furious fool." It was wise in him, then, to re-enter the public arena by a side door, and to shelter himself in the shadow of a corner.

The genius of Gambetta soon surmounted the ephemeral obloquy under which he rested. Already he had won the renown of being the very first among living French orators; and this was saying much, at a time when Thiers, Victor Hugo, Jules Favre, and Louis Blanc were yet alive. He had also proved himself a great organizer and administrator, despite his inevitable failure. But hitherto he had exhibited only tremendous energy, headlong rashness, extreme opinion, and a hot and impetuously partisan method of urging it. His head was strong, but had not been thought "level." As a politician and party leader he was as yet untried. His eloquence

was sure to be a power; his magnetic influence
over men would inevitably make him a considerable personage in the Assembly. But had he
tact, judgment, resource, in party warfare? When
he reappeared at Versailles there was not probably a man in France who did not regard him
as a radical of radicals; an irreconcilable, perhaps a socialist, possibly a friend of the commune. Thiers counted on his violent hostility;
and the old statesman, for once not shrewd, con-
temned his opposition.

It is not too much to say that within three
years after Gambetta, bearing such a character
as has been described, had taken his seat in the
Assembly, he had proved himself the ablest and
most consummate party chief in the France of
this century. So far from turning out to be a
"furious fool," incapable of self-control, impracticable, revolutionary, hot-headed, and vindictive,
Gambetta — and Gambetta alone — gathered the
discordant factions of the republican party into
a compact and harmonious body, reconciled their
differences, patched up their personal quarrels,
soothed their contending ambitions, made them
a united army crusading for a great and practicable cause, and himself led them to one of the

most memorable political victories ever won.
He was a wonderful magician in his use of party
tactics. He restrained or let loose the ardor of
his followers at will, each at the moment when
restraint or when display would be most effective
for the end in view. His resources in the fencing
and manœuvring of the parliamentary struggle ·
were simply inexhaustible. His temper, self-restraint, presence of mind, rapidity of decision,
tact, and ingenuity; his masterly management of
the monarchial opposition; the faith in his honesty, his aims, and his methods, with which he
inspired not only the republican rank and file,
but stubborn minds like those of Thiers, Re-
musat, and Dufaure; his ceaseless activity, his
absorbing pursuit of the great end in view — the
secure establishment of the republic — betrayed
that his genius for party leadership was not less
conspicuous than his genius for eloquence and
for vigorous administration.

The republic, indeed, as it is to-day, owes its
very existence more to Gambetta than to any
other one man. Step by step he won advan-
tages in the Assembly over a bitter monarchical
majority. He made the utmost of the dissen-
sions of the monarchists among themselves;

forced them to proclaim the republic because
nothing else could be agreed upon; compelled
them to actually elect a majority of republican
life senators among the seventy-five to be chosen
by the Assembly. Temporarily discomfited by
the resignation of Thiers and the election of the
monarchist MacMahon to the Presidency, Gambetta carried on his party warfare with so much
vigor and wisdom that he rendered MacMahon
helpless, and developed the fact that France had
become republican to the core of its heart.

When, early in 1879, MacMahon found himself at last compelled to resign, Gambetta, had
he chosen, might have secured the Presidency as
the Marshal's successor. But, with that keen
and wise foresight for which he is remarkable,
he saw that the time was not yet ripe; and,
with the same patriotic self-abnegation with
which, in 1871, he had laid absolute power at
the feet of the Assembly, he now turned away
from the glittering prize which might easily have
been his. He accepted, instead (to the surprise
of most men), the chair of the Chamber of
Deputies. It has almost seemed as if Gambetta,
throughout his romantic public career, had desired to show the world how wide is the *versatility*

of his talents; to prove himself brilliantly capable in many capacities. As has already been said, his conduct as the presiding officer of the most turbulent assemblage in the world has been, by universal confession, conspicuously able. He has sustained the dignity as well as enforced the power of the chair. He has compelled respect from his bitterest and most violent enemies; and he has guided business and debate in such a manner as to secure every deputy his right, and every interest of the nation its hearing.

Gambetta has proved himself to be, in his later career, anything but an impracticable radical. This is shown, if by nothing else, by the fact that he succeeded in winning the confidence of Thiers, while he has shaken that of the extremists, Victor Hugo and Louis Blanc. The thoroughly practical character, not only of his party leadership, but of his statesmanship, has been amply demonstrated over and over again during the past seven difficult years. He has supported moderate men and measures, and adopted moderate methods. He is, as he always has been from early youth up, a republican to the heart's core. He waged uncompromising warfare, first upon the second empire, then upon the Bonapartism, Legitimism, and Orleanism of the Assembly. He has devoted herculean labors to the establishment of the republic. There can be no sort of doubt of his sincerity and ardor in its cause. But to class him as a socialist or a communist, to suspect him of rash schemes, of visionary projects, to imagine that he would introduce into the republic the maxims of Proudhon or the ideas of Marat, is to utterly misread his career. There is every reason to suppose that Gambetta sees in the conservative democracy of the United States his ideal of a free government. He would have the central power strong enough to preserve order and to dispense equal justice to all. While no French statesman is more emphatic in his denunciations of a political and educating church, Gambetta is far from seeking to inspire a crusade against religion. He would place every church on an equal footing, and equally exclude every church from the domain of politics. He would have the public education of France purely secular. In these opinions he is at one with many leading and by no means revolutionary English liberals, and agrees with Americans of a conservative type. At first suspected of a secret sympathy with the commune, Gambetta soon purged himself of that suspicion. He upheld Thiers in his measures against the insurrection, and even in the numerous executions on the field of Satory. Later he has opposed that complete amnesty for which eloquent radicals like Louis Blanc have clamored. He supported the cabinet of the ex-Orleanist Dufaure, and still more heartily has sustained that of the more liberal Waddington. Indeed, Gambetta has for several years held the fate of ministries in the palm of his hand. By a signal of his finger he might at any moment have overthrown Dufaure; Waddington or de Freycinet could not have remained Premier a day but for the sufferance of the great republican chief. Ambition might have prompted Gambetta more than once to act the part of a cabinet-maker; but his devotion to the republic, and his keen perception of the necessity of compromise, of the utility of stooping to conquer, has always held his personal aspirations in effectual check.

In personal characteristics, Gambetta is in many respects as simple and democratic as he was in the old impecunious days, when he inhabited the Paris Bohemia, and vainly awaited briefs. At that time, however, the out-at-elbows student and lawyer was, we fear, a roisterer and reveller. The stories of his escapades and dissipation, of the orgies of which he was the stormy spirit, and the lawlessness of the offending of which he was the head and front, still float about the clubs and *cafés*. He was rather idle, reckless, fond of noisy pleasures, lavish when he had that with which to lavish, and apparently fast travelling a down-hill road. In these respects, at least, he was made a new man by his sudden leap into fame. Politics often have a reforming influence upon dissipated young men of brains. It is said that the Marquis of Hartington, recently the leader of the English Liberal party, and one of the soundest and most respected of English statesmen, was weaned from headlong dissipation by the firing of his soul with political ambition. His father compelled him to go into the House of Commons; and the prizes which there glittered before his eyes sobered him for life. In like manner Gambetta seems to have been sobered and purified by finding that, by an hour's speech, he had awakened the admiration and homage of France. He was then thirty years of age; young enough to have his head turned, and to convert his recklessness into almost equally ruinous conceit. But Gambetta was not spoiled by sudden, dazzling, intoxicating success. He did not even play the part of Henry V., and discard his old roistering boon companions. For some time after, he was still the loud-tongued oracle of the Café Procope. With fees now coming in plentifully, as a substantial fruit of his quick fame, he still lived modestly, in an upper apartment of the musty Latin quarter, and did not put on any airs. It may be that the celebrated little white flower, always now to be seen in his button-hole, first made its appearance there in the dawn of his prosperous days. Otherwise, alike in dress, and in democracy of manner, he continued to be, as he had been, unostentatious and simple.

Gambetta remained a poor man throughout his deputyship, his dictatorship, and his long career in the Assembly and afterwards in the Chamber. No taint of corruptibility or dishonesty ever clung to his skirts. He might easily have become a millionaire, by not very wide departures from the recognized code of political morality; but down to the time that he moved into the palace set apart for the President of the Chamber, his mode of life was that of a man in very moderate circumstances. It is well known, too, that he is not thrifty; that he spends freely what he gets. He is not of the saving sort. After his instalment in the Presidential palace, he displayed such show and ostentation as he thinks befitting the dignity of the second office of the republic in point of importance. The receptions he gave, indeed, rivalled in brilliancy those of President Grévy. He has always shown himself a genial and graceful host, and his style of hospitality would not have disgraced one born in the purple of hereditary rank.

His daily life as a legislative prince — this Bohemian son of a rustic tradesman — gives an insight into his personal traits. Like many Frenchmen, he is a late riser. He takes a cup of coffee and a roll in bed, then gets up, reads the morning papers, and goes through the large pile of letters that await him. At ten o'clock he envelops his portly form in a long dressing-gown, and passes into a small cabinet, where he receives the crowd of satellites and friends who daily make it a point to pay their court to the most powerful man in France.

" The moment the conversation becomes interesting," says *Figaro*, describing the scene, " the door opens quietly, and a man with a severe

countenance enters with a card. 'All right,' says
Gambetta, 'I am coming down;' and he tries
to continue the conversation. But the man,
placid and implacable, remains till his master has
changed his dressing-gown for a more solemn
attire. He does not withdraw till Gambetta
leaves the room. From this moment Gambetta
devotes himself body and soul to politics. It is
in vain that Louis, at eleven o'clock, announces
that breakfast is served. The breakfast must
wait. At length, when Gambetta tries to relish
a couple of fried eggs, his favorite dish, the
severe-looking man again presents himself, like a
statue, with card in hand. First of all, Gambetta
tries not to see this household Banquo. He
buries his nose in his plate. But the man is not
to be balked; and, presenting the card with one
hand, and pointing majestically to the name it
bears with the other, he still stands firm at his
master's side. This means something serious,
and Gambetta obeys Banquo. Who is this mysterious person? He is Père Dumangin, an old
republican — the watch-dog, reminder, the time-
piece of his master and friend. When Dumangin
has spoken, the matter is settled. Gambetta receives only those who please Dumangin."

Gambetta is a bachelor; but he has not lived

so long without having at least contemplated marriage. The story of his engagement to an heiress in western France, and its sudden breaking-off, give us a fresh glimpse of his character. From the time of his leaving his humble home at Cahors, till his rise to the highest rank of public personages, Gambetta lived with a faithful, loving, devoted aunt, who had followed him to Paris, and who made, everywhere he went, a pleasant home for him. She was at once his maid-of-all-work and his congenial companion; and he was as deeply attached to her as she to him. His engagement to a handsome and accomplished girl, with a dowry of seven millions, was a shock to the good aunt; but she yielded gracefully to the inevitable. When the arrangements for the marriage were being discussed, however, the young lady took it into her head to make it a condition of their union that the aunt should be excluded from the new establishment. She was scarcely elegant enough to adorn gilded *salons*. Gambetta explained how much his aunt had been to him; the rich beauty was only the more obdurate. Gambetta took up his hat, and with a profound bow, "Adieu," said he; "we were not made to understand each other." And the marriage was put off forever.

At the early age of forty-one, Gambetta may be said to stand midway in a career, which, if closed now, would be regarded as one of the most striking, romantic and successful in the annals of political biography. He must already be confessed to be a great orator, an able practical administrator, a consummate party leader, a statesman fertile in resources, a presiding officer of rare vigor, tact, and mastery over public assemblies. A brilliant future seems to lie before him. Aside from his eminent capacity, his services to the republic, which owes its existence to him more than to any one man, entitle him to its highest honors when the fitting time shall come. The vicissitudes of public life in France are well expressed by the epigram, that in that country " nothing is probable except the unforeseen." It may be that the greatest of living Frenchmen will miss the Presidency, as in this country did Webster and Clay. But all present indications point to the probability that ere Gambetta passes the ripe prime of middle age, he will be elevated to the seat already so eminently adorned by Adolph Thiers and Jules Grévy, and which he is fitted to adorn none the less than they.

IV.

BEACONSFIELD.

THE romance of politics contains no more strange and striking chapter than the story of the career of Benjamin Disraeli, Earl of Beaconsfield. It is not improbable that that career is already rounded and finished. Lord Beaconsfield is in his seventy-fifth year. He has retired from a long and perplexing tenure of power; a power embracing the sway of a vast and mighty Empire, and which must have tried the mental energies and the physical strength of a man young and hale. But Lord Beaconsfield's health has for years been feeble, and more than once his life has seemed imperilled by his exhausting labors. It is little likely, therefore, that he will resume the rule which he held with such bold and audacious purpose for the six years between 1874 and 1880. What years he has yet to live will perhaps be spent in the august repose of the House of Peers; that house in which he still seems out of place, almost an intruder, yet in which he has achieved some of his most notable triumphs of eloquence and statecraft.

This supposably rounded romance, therefore, may be observed as a whole; and so looking at it, we cannot but be struck by its similarity to the romance of the skilful novelist, in the crowning glories of its ending. At the outset, we see a young, gay, gilded dandy, who has written some very queer novels of society, is petted by the half-aristocratic, half-Bohemian circle of Gore House, is a curiosity as an Anglicized Jew, has wit and fine manners, is strikingly handsome, and altogether a bright and breezy presence in a drawing-room. Everybody sees that he has a perfectly imperturbable audacity, that he proposes to make his way in the fashionable, not less than in the literary, world; but few suspect, at first, that he dreams of political distinction. His grandfather was a kindly and hospitable old Italian Jew, who used to give neat suppers to men of note at Enfield. His father was a bookish scholar, full of literary research and anecdote, a quiet but genial old man, who lived in pleasant simplicity in Bloomsbury. No one imagined that a gay young fop, with the despised Hebrew blood in his veins, could aim higher than the pleasure of being a momentary lion among the West End fashionables. To be fêted as the author of "Vivian Grey," to be admired for the exquisite cut of his coats, the sparkle of his jewelry, and the harmonious colors of his cravat and waistcoat — these seemed to be the bounds of his ambition.

Yet had that superficially reading West End coterie, where he was so pleasantly welcomed, perused with more care and insight the novels concerning which they so generously flattered him, they might have discovered between the lines an ambition far loftier and more arrogant. This truth gradually dawned upon his circle as novel after novel, and then satire after satire, appeared from his pen; each of which took on a more and more distinct political hue. But almost before it became recognized that his attention was directed to politics, he suddenly appeared as a candidate for the House of Commons. With "sentiments which were Tory, and presentiments which were Radical," he boldly contested the borough of High Wycombe with no less an antagonist than a brother of Earl Grey, then prime minister of England. Defeated there, a few months later he again

appeared in the field, only to suffer, first at
Marylebone, and then at Taunton, two more dis-
comfitures. Not a whit daunted, he made a
further struggle to win a seat in Parliament, and
this time, aided by powerful friends, he at last
succeeded, being chosen in 1837 a member by
the borough of Maidstone. Soon after this triumph, he was introduced to Lord Melbourne,
who had now become Prime Minister. Lord
Melbourne looked at the gorgeously attired
young legislator, with his glistening curls and his
large, bright black eye, with a feeling of mingled
amusement and curiosity. "What do you wish
to be?" he asked him. "Prime Minister of
England, my lord," was the startling and audacious reply. Lord Melbourne thought the an-
swer an epigram. Disraeli expressed in it the
whole volume of his political ambition.

It is not at all my purpose to follow Benjamin
Disraeli through that brilliant and energetic
career, each step of which, as now appears,
brought him nearer the lofty goal upon which
his eyes were ever fixed. His first ignominious
failure, when he rose to address his maiden
speech to the House; his patient waiting to re-
cover from its effect; his oratorical triumph on

the occasion of his second attempt; his quarrel with Sir Robert Peel, in which he exhausted every resource of the bitterest invective to overwhelm the Tory leader with humiliation; his passages-at-arms with O'Connell; his audacity in seizing upon the Tory leadership; the surprise with which England rubbed her eyes and stared to see him her chancellor of the exchequer; his long-continued and magnificent forensic combats with Gladstone; his ascent to the premiership in 1868, and his courageous gift of household suffrage to the people; his later triumphs as premier; his promotion to the House of Lords as Earl of Beaconsfield, and his assumption of the envied insignia of Knight of the Garter; these are history, and oft-repeated history, a tale told, especially of late, with copious iteration, and with every degree of friendly panegyric and of hostile criticism.

But such a man, with a career so strange, an origin so alien and despised, and triumphs so entirely without parallel in English political annals, must always be an extremely interesting study. It is safe to say that no English statesman, remote or modern, has been the subject of so many diverse surmises and theories, has been so difficult to read and interpret, or has given rise to so many utterly contradictory estimates, both as to moral and intellectual qualities, as Benjamin Disraeli. He is scarcely less of a riddle now, when he has been in the full blaze of public notoriety for forty years, than he was the day that he entered the House, with confident, dainty, and dandified step, tripping across its historic floor. There are many thousands of people in England to whom he is the great figure of the age; who trust him, admire him with unbounded enthusiasm, unquestioningly follow him in paths however mysterious, and believe alike in his statesmanship and in his sincerity. There are other thousands to whom he is as utterly odious, who look upon him as a political Mephistopheles, a theatric poser in statesmanship, a charlatan, absolutely selfish and devoid of moral feeling, who would with untroubled heart sacrifice England and Englishmen to triumph in a policy and to retain a hold on power.

The first time that I saw Benjamin Disraeli, now Earl of Beaconsfield and Knight of the Garter, was in the House of Commons, in the early summer of 1863. It was a period when the relations between England and the United States were, to say the least, somewhat strained.

The Peterhoff matter had well-nigh brought the two countries to an actual rupture. A week before I had been at Oxford, and one night, in one of the many cosey inns of the ancient university city, I had heard college proctors talking excitedly about a speech that Palmerston had just made, foreshadowing war with America. Palmerston was then prime minister, Gladstone was his chancellor of the exchequer, Lord Derby was the Tory leader, and Disraeli was his faithful and brilliant lieutenant in the House of Commons. It was on a memorable night in the House that I first visited that famous assembly. Gladstone was to make one of his greatest efforts in favor of taxing the great, rich public charities. House, lobby, and galleries were crowded. It was interesting to observe, for the first time, the distinguished assemblage which was and is really the governing power of the great British Empire. It was yet more interesting to hear the consummate orator of the Liberals, with his clear, silvery, persuasive voice, pleading that Christ's Hospital and other rich charitable corporations should assume their share of the financial burdens of the state. But most interesting was it, to me at least, to look along the crowded benches which hung on the chancellor's words with breathless interest, and to note the faces and bearing of the famous men who composed the chief adornments of the body and of British statesmanship.

And to me, the most remarkable and striking face and figure of all, were those of him who sat, almost alone, in the very centre of the front opposition bench, whose hat was well jammed down over his eyes, who sat motionless from the beginning to the end of Gladstone's speech, and who seemed rather to be in a deep reverie, or perhaps half-asleep, than attentive to what was going forward in the House. Now and then the hat would be removed for a few moments from the head; and then I had an ample opportunity to observe the features of the man who, all things considered, had even then reached the position of the most successful politician of his age.

Let me describe him as he appeared at the age of fifty-seven. The first impression was of his wonderful youthfulness. At the distance where he sat from the Speaker's Gallery, he looked scarcely more than thirty; and his attire served to confirm this impression. A black coat,

buttoned tightly at the waist; an immaculate
shirt bosom; a carefully tied necktie; large,
light-gray trousers, cut in the nick of the fashion;
hair glossily black and curly, betraying the
scrupulous care with which each particular curl
must have been arranged in its place; large,
rather dreamy, and indifferent black eyes; a
thick, heavy, Jewish nose; a large mouth, with
thick, colorless lips; a longish chin, covered
with a tuft of gray-black beard; a sallow complexion, almost deathly sallow; a strong, well-
knit, rather high-shouldered figure; these were
the external features that attracted the cursory
glance of the eye. It has been said that Disraeli,
leader and chieftain as he is, has always seemed
a man alone and apart from his colleagues; so
un-English that he has not been able to fuse with
the rest; solitary amid all the hurly-burly bustle
of politics; keeping himself within himself; with
few or no ardent bosom friends; amiable, patient,
and courteous, perhaps, but maintaining a distance between himself and his most intimate
advisers. Looking down upon him as he sat in
the House, this theory appeared to be confirmed
by superficial observation. He sat alone, with a
space between him and the next man on either

side. It was very rarely that he turned to speak to this or that one; then, the conversation seemed almost monosyllabic. It was evident, to say the least, that he was not a chatty man like Palmerston, nor a vehement talker like Gladstone. Closer scrutiny made it apparent, however, that he was far from indifferent about what was going forward. A quiet smile crossed his face as Gladstone, now and then, went rather out of his way to direct a shaft of sarcasm at his own breast; and when, an hour or two after, Disraeli rose to take his share in the debate, it soon became clear that all that had been before said had been carefully fixed in his mind. This imperturbability and apparent unconsciousness of what is going forward, whether it be affectation or temperament, has always struck lookers-on in the House of Lords and Commons. " However fierce the debate," says one of them, "or heated the House, or pressing the crisis, there sits Disraeli, occasionally looking at his hands, or the clock; otherwise, silent, unmoved, and still. Yet an Indian scout could not keep a more vigilant watch; and immediately an opportunity occurs he is on his legs, boiling with real or affected indignation."

There never spoke an orator more curious and interesting to observe, more puzzling to estimate, more entertaining to study. After the House had been filled and was still echoing with the silvery vehemence and trembling earnestness of Gladstone's voice, it was indeed a very abrupt contrast to listen to the more quiet, more studied, more even and steadily sustained and carefully poised periods of his rival. If Disraeli's first speech in the House forty years ago was the very bathos of attempted melodramatic force, the histrionic air and study of effect have at least never since been lost. It is clear that in his own un-English and unexampled style, Disraeli is a parliamentary speaker of the first rank. He never thrills an audience to generous enthusiasm, like Bright; nor has he the strong capacity of Gladstone to strike conviction pressing home to the minds of those who listen to him. But he is superior to either in making a perfectly clear, brief, yet exhaustive parliamentary statement. In the literary perfection, the variety, the polish of his style, it would be hard to point out his equal. His self-possession and self-command never desert him. He never really loses his head in fine frenzies of passion, though it is sometimes his cue to appear to do so. As you listen to him, you cannot but feel that this singular and effective eloquence is the product of long and patient self-training; that it is the outcome of a lengthened devotion to oratory as an art; and that this art has been studied with an especial view to its use in the British House of Commons. Adroitness in the management alike of thought and phrases, is a trait speedily recognized. Each is suited precisely to the speaker's purpose for the moment. If that purpose is to lash an antagonist into a fury, or to divert him from the issue, you will have a quick succession of sparkling epigrams and barbed shafts of ridicule. Disraeli is a master of all the tortures supplied by the armory of rhetoric. For years he was able, almost at will, to sting Gladstone out of his self-control; and it was always a source of extreme irritation to Gladstone, that he could never produce a like effect upon his rival. Indeed, Disraeli has always had a habit of rather obtrusively showing the House that he was perfect master of himself when " on his legs." It has been related that on one occasion, when in the midst of a long and important speech, he stopped, took an orange from his pocket, punched a hole in it with his knife, and began deliberately to suck it; and continued to do so at intervals during the rest of his address. There are many peculiarities of manner, each of which seems to have been artistically fixed upon beforehand, as if to produce its especial result. Invariably, when he rises to speak, he wears a slight smile, which seems to hint that the arguments on the other side, specious as they seem, are not overwhelming, and are about to be effectively answered. There is a saucy gleam of the black eye, too, which lends aid to the significance of the smile. His speech is full of rhetorical "hits;" each hit is accompanied by gestures extremely expressive, and by a measuring of the tones of the voice so as to produce surprise and instant effect. A grimace or a shrug of the shoulders will give "point" to the epigram; and when it has thus been delivered, Disraeli alone in the assemblage will preserve an impassive face, while every one is laughing and cheering around him. At other times he ascends to greater heights in the art of eloquence. He can evidently warm up at will; many of his flights of simile, or appeals, or apostrophes, are so flowery that they come to the very verge of bombast,

and escape by the narrowest line from passing
into bathos; but the line is never, in these later
and riper years, actually crossed. A happy turn,
a fine finishing off, always saves the rhapsody,
and makes it effective. Disraeli certainly has
more humor than either of the two orators who
have so long disputed the palm with him. Gladstone, indeed, has no humor, and that of Bright
is somewhat grim and puritanic. The Tory chief
has clearly made as much of a study of humor
as of any other rhetorical weapon. To quote
again the writer before cited, " he has made
himself master of the greatest weakness of the
House of Commons — its love of a good laugh."
No living English orator has said so many good
things, applied so many apt epithets, that have
" stuck." His happy phrases, his well-considered
jests, upon the various characters of the House
in which the greater part of his political career
was spent, are eagerly enjoyed still, and are more
numerous than those uttered by any other pro-
fessed wit in politics. In describing Gladstone
recently, as a " sophistical rhetorician, drowned
in the exuberance of his own verbosity," he came
just near enough the truth to make a telling hit,
and thereby did more to confirm Tory animosity

towards the Liberal leader, than if he had exhausted hours in elaborate denunciation of him. Many of his neat little personal witticisms are still afloat, and are repeated whenever the names of the victims of them are mentioned. The "Batavian grace" of Mr. Beresford Hope's manner, the "want of finish" in Lord Salisbury's invective, the description of Goldwin Smith as "an itinerant spouter of stale sedition," Sergeant Dowse's "jovial profligacy," will long be repeated with appreciative chuckles in the region of the Pall Mall clubs, and in the centres of Tory reunions. There is not a single Liberal leader whom Disraeli has not labelled with some apt and witty designation, which has clung and will always cling to him, as long as he is a figure of British politics. Disraeli has shown, too, that he can wield the force of fierce invective quite as vigorously as he can lighten the prosy proceedings of parliament by airy and not ill-natured humor. His onslaughts on Sir Robert Peel were as cruel and ferocious as they were powerful and effective.

When on his feet, Disraeli is more liberal in gesture than most parliamentary speakers. He uses his hands and arms freely, and often sways

his body forward, as if bowing. His voice is
neither harsh nor musical. It has neither the
persuasive tones of Gladstone, nor the grating
sounds produced by Lord Russell, Lord Lytton,
and some other English orators. He seldom
hesitates for a word; but sometimes appears to
do so, evidently to increase the effect of what
follows. No English public man probably more
carefully prepares his speeches. There is ample
evidence of study and polish in each of them.
He is never so happy in a debate suddenly
sprung upon him, as on a field night when one
party delivers deliberate battle to the other. Let
it be added that advancing age and persistent
ill health do not seem to have diminished his
oratorical powers. His last speech in the House
of Lords, before the dissolution of the parliament
which he so long and so completely swayed, was
as audacious, vigorous, and brilliant as any he
has delivered for years. It bristled with bold
statement, bright epigram, and energetic defiance. He has always been a better after-dinner
speaker than Gladstone; for his gifts as an orator
incline him to delight in the lighter and airier
graces of the art, while Gladstone is ever too
dead-in-earnest to use or cultivate them. Dis-

racli's speeches at the dinners of the Royal Academy, and at the annual feasts of the Lord Mayor in the Guildhall, will long be remembered for their cheery grace and pungent wit.

Disraeli's statesmanship will no doubt be a subject of warm difference of opinion among Englishmen. His inconsistency, in the earlier years of his public life, in passing rapidly from a strange sort of Oriental radicalism into the *ultima thule* of Tory belief, and in outdoing any other Tory leader in his denunciations of Sir Robert Peel for an apostasy prompted by patriotism, is still bitterly criticised by his Liberal rivals, especially by those Liberals who were once Peel's devoted followers. His attempts to restore protection as the economic policy of England, after accepting the dogma of free trade, are still remembered. Perhaps nothing that he ever did more completely disturbed the equanimity of his opponents than his sudden adoption of household suffrage as the basis of a sweeping electoral reform. The Liberals had tried in vain for years to frame a reform bill that would be acceptable to the House and the country. They had lost power in 1866 by offering a moderate and well-considered measure. They regarded electoral reform as their special mission and function. It never entered their heads that on their own ground they would be distanced by a Tory chief, followed by a Tory party. But no sooner had Disraeli found himself in office than, as he himself afterwards airily boasted at Edinburgh, he began "to educate his party." It was no common triumph of political tactics to bring the stolid Tory squires and the proud Tory lords to assent to a sweeping extension of the suffrage; and it is safe to say that Disraeli was the only living politician who could have done it, or who would even have been bold enough to try. To "steal the thunder of the Whigs," however, was quite in harmony with his audacious, adventurous nature; nor could those who admired Peel, for doing precisely the same thing in the matter of the corn laws, very loudly blame him. Whatever may be thought of his later foreign policy, there can be no doubt that the accomplishment of household suffrage, which was Disraeli's own work, and in a large measure his personal victory, was an act producing great and most beneficial results. Were his political fame to rest upon that alone, it is difficult to see how future generations, at least, can deny him the title to effective and substantial statesmanship. The household suffrage reform extended the suffrage to thousands of the lower classes; and for this reason the obstacles in the way of Disraeli's being able to induce the Tories to accept it were tremendous. By patience, by tact, by appeal to the ambition for party victory, and by sheer pluck, he overcame them. He predicted, amid the jeers of his opponents, that among the working classes there was a strong Tory substratum. The prediction, strangely as it sounded, was fulfilled when, in 1874, the new electorate carried Disraeli into power by an overwhelming vote.

Then began a new and much more thrilling chapter in the record of his public acts. For the first time, he presided over a cabinet which was supported by an ample, compact, and submissive majority in both Houses of Parliament. His rule was unfettered and unobstructed. From the beginning, it was clear that his bold spirit and strong individuality constituted the central and controlling force of the administration. He had no rival in influence in his cabinet. One and all were his subordinates and followers. It was emphatically his policy which was pursued throughout the long and perplexing crisis of the Eastern Question in its later phase; and those of the cabinet — Lords Derby and Carnarvon — who would not follow his policy to the end, never thought of contesting his authority in that body, but retired from it. One of Disraeli's most remarkable feats, in recent years, has been his conversion of the proud, irritable, and arrogant Marquis of Salisbury from an inveterate personal foe into a warm friend and a submissive adherent.

Despite the "un-English" reputation which many writers have succeeded in giving Disraeli, it can scarcely be questioned that his Eastern policy was thoroughly English in its precedents and bearing. He seems to have closely followed in the footsteps of Wellington, Peel, and Palmerston. The corner-stone of the English policy in regard to the Eastern Question has been for fifty years the principle that, in order to check the aggression of Russia, Turkey must be preserved, defended, and propped up. Even the Liberals, including Gladstone and Granville, adhered to this principle at the time of the Crimean war, and have only within a few years drifted away from it. It animated Disraeli's course throughout. Whether effectually or not — this is a matter still to be decided by the lapse of time

and the current of events — he steadily labored
to preserve as far as possible the power of the
Sultan, and to curb as far as possible the power
of the Czar. He resolved, moreover, that England should no longer hold aloof, as she had
done in the days of Liberal ascendancy, from
participation in continental politics. She should
resume her old place as an active and self-assert-
ing great power. Her voice should be heard in
the Areopagi of nations, her influence felt in
every international concern. "The honor and
power of the Empire," this was the brave shib-
boleth often heard in his mouth and the mouths
of his colleagues. It was the counterpart to the
Liberal motto of "Retrenchment and Reform;"
and long sounded more sweetly in the people's
ears.

Success has attended Disraeli's efforts, at least
so far as to bring England once more into active
relations with other powers, and to give her a
more commanding voice in the direction of
European events. This result he brought about
by bold and often surprising and theatrical
courses. The creation of the title of Empress of
India, the purchase of the Suez Canal shares,
the importation of Hindoo troops into the Medi-

terranean, the entrance of the British fleet into
the Dardanelles, and the acquisition of Cyprus,
were acts the wisdom of which has to be proved
by the sequence of events yet to occur, but
which, there can be no doubt, were resolute and
striking strokes of statesmanship. Whether Disraeli's Eastern policy, or that of his successors,
will prove to be the best for the preservation of
the British Empire, remains still a problem to be
solved by the future.

In one statesmanlike quality — in sagacious
foresight — no American, at least, ought to un-
derestimate Disraeli's abilities. Whatever his
motive, he, almost alone of English statesmen of
either party, favored the cause of the North in
our civil war, and steadily, even at the darkest
periods, predicted its final triumph. When Gladstone was eulogizing Jefferson Davis, and declar-
ing that he had made " an independent nation ; "
when Sir John Ramsden was exultingly boasting
that " the republican bubble had burst;" when
Palmerston was plotting with the Emperor Napoleon, with a view to a recognition of the
Southern confederacy; when Lord John Russell
was asserting that the war was one " for empire
on one side and independence on the other ; "

when Lords Derby and Cranbourne (the latter now Marquis of Salisbury) were hotly declaiming against the arrogance of the North in attempting to preserve the Union, Benjamin Disraeli saw the right, and foresaw the victory. The friendly feeling he displayed towards us throughout the war found most eloquent expression in noble speech, when the assassination of Lincoln thrilled Europe as well as America, with its dreadful shock.

" In the character of the victim," he declared, " and even in the accessories of his last moments, there is something so homely and so innocent, that it takes, as it were, the subject out of the pomp of history and the ceremonial of diplomacy; it touches the heart of nations, and appeals to the domestic sentiment of mankind."

Then, after showing that the assassination of rulers seldom changes the history of mankind, and remarking that Lincoln had "fulfilled his duty with simplicity and strength," he thus closed one of the most moving and evidently heart-felt addresses he ever made : —

" In expressing our unaffected and profound sympathy with the citizens of the United States at the untimely end of their elected chief, let us not, therefore, sanction any feeling of depression;

but rather let us express a fervent hope that from out of the awful trials of the last four years, of which not the least is this violent demise, the various populations of North America may issue elevated and chastened, rich in that accumulated wisdom and strong in that disciplined energy which a young nation can only acquire in a protracted and perilous struggle. Then they will be enabled not only to renew their career of power and prosperity, but they will renew it to contribute to the general happiness of mankind."

Whatever may be thought of the wisdom, in many respects, of Disraeli's career as a practical statesman, there can be but one opinion as to his genius for party leadership. Herein he presents a very suggestive contrast to Gladstone. Not even Palmerston, with all his *bonhomie* and faculty for conciliation, was Disraeli's equal in this respect. The English government is organically one of party. No statesman can be completely successful unless he is a skilful party leader; and this leadership demands a combination of qualities which it is not very frequent to find combined. No situation more emphatically needs a command of exhaustless patience, perseverance, and pluck; and these qualities Disraeli showed that he possessed, to a remarkable degree, at a very early period of his public career. Never had a party chief more formidable difficulties with which to contend. The party which he aspired to lead, and upon whom he fairly fixed his leadership by making his brilliant talents absolutely necessary to it, was, of all parties, that whose prejudices were deepest against his race, and whose contempt of *parvenus* and self-made men was the most inveterate. Yet he took this obstinate and haughty party in hand, drilled, massed, and " educated " it, and so fashioned its line of action that he brought it into power and sustained it there. He became the irresistible leader of a compact and submissive party organization, which has acted for many years under his inspiration with the discipline, precision, and force of a thoroughly trained army. Throughout the period of his Tory chiefship he has maintained an even and unruffled patience, a constant good temper, and an unflagging persistency. Thoroughly capable in this branch of leadership, he has been able to supplement it in parliament by his consummate skill in debate, his resources as an orator, and his adroitness in party tactics; by his audacity in attack, and his

ever ready and equal courage in orderly retreat;
by his sagacity in marking out plans of parliamentary campaigns, his assiduous cultivation of
the younger and rising talents in his ranks, and
the inexhaustible fertility of his resources in the
most bitterly contested party battles. For years
it has been recognized that no other Tory chief
was possible while Disraeli lived and remained
in public life. Many a time he with difficulty
saved the party from the consequences of Lord
Derby's rashness, and the timidity and narrow-
ness of his lieutenants. In the cabinet, he alone
could have formed the connecting bond which
so long held statesmen so diverse in temperament and opinion as the Marquis of Salisbury
and Sir Stafford Northcote, Gathorne Hardy and
the present Lord Derby. In the art of conciliation, there never was a more consummate adept;
he has known how to smooth over irritated
susceptibilities, to soothe ruffled pride, to soften
down bitter prejudices, and to smother threatened
revolt, with a hand at once gentle and firm, and
the influence of a suavity which not more
charmed than it imposed the will which prompted
it. The Tory party of this generation cannot
hope to secure such another leader. If he retires,

content with his earldom, his Garter, his triumph at Berlin, and the proud consciousness of having for six years brilliantly ruled the mighty Empire of Britain, it is highly probable that his party must abide for years in the old shade of opposition; for the near future, at least, seems to be secured to the Liberals, to whose power a consummate Tory leader alone would be dangerous.

The same sparkle of social wit and bright epigram which makes Disraeli so attractive an after-dinner speaker, gives him popularity in the amenities of private life. Amid all the turmoil and cares of a long and stirring public career, he has never lost the talent of making himself agreeable in society, which he so carefully cultivated in the days of his youth. Essentially a courtier, he has made himself especially agreeable to the Queen and the royalties; and he is a welcome guest in those country-house gatherings which are so delightful a feature of English social life. He is an elegant and graceful host; and alien as he is called, he has contrived to become thoroughly and aristocratically English in this regard. In the fine old manor of Hughenden, in Buckinghamshire, he entertains royal princes and ministerial colleagues with equal suavity and

genial manner; yet, with all his aptitude and
talent for society, he seems most often — especially since his wife's death — to prefer solitude,
amid his books and papers, with the sole companionship of one who is at once his most intimate friend and his private secretary.[1] For the
national sports of Englishmen, Disraeli appears
to have little taste. It is rarely that he follows
the hounds to the hunt, or shows himself on the
world-famous racing grounds; nor does he incline to such methods of violent physical exercise
as delight his great rival, Gladstone. On the
other hand, he is known in his own neighbor-
hood as a model landlord. Considerate towards
his tenantry, entering with zest into the interests
of the farms, making his appearance familiarly
at the harvest-homes, Disraeli thus sets an example to those English landed magnates who
desert their acres for the pleasures of the great
capitals. His married life, though he married a
lady some years older than himself, was a very
happy one throughout its duration of forty years.
There was something touching and noble in the
way in which he always referred to her in his
public addresses. His constant and chivalrous

---

[1] Montagu Corry, now Lord Rowton.

devotion to her was often remarked. Once he spoke of her, in a speech at Hughenden, as the "best wife in England;" he dedicated his romance, "Sibyl," to "the most severe of critics, but a perfect wife;" he declared, in an address in Scotland, that it was to her encouragement and support that he owed his eminence. When the Queen offered him a peerage on one occasion, he declined it, and begged that if any such honor were to be conferred, it should be upon Mrs. Disraeli; who thereupon was created Viscountess Beaconsfield. Her death, a year or two before his second premiership, seemed to overwhelm him with a grief from which he has perhaps never quite recovered.

In closing this rapid study of the remarkable man whose name has been so often in men's mouths during the past six years, I quote what was recently and truly said of him by one of his admiring fellow-countrymen : —

"His career is a romance; but it is a romance that teaches a thousand useful and noble lessons, that will have power, in times when the party passions of to-day shall be cold, to fire many a young soul with the highest ambition, and to fill many a tender heart with sympathy for him whose story it records."

V.

CASTELAR.

WHAT is to be the fate of the Latin nations of southern Europe, is an interesting and curious problem. Are they even now sinking, more or less gradually, into decrepitude and decay? Is the great part played by the Latin races in the world nearly played out? Has empire in war and letters passed away forever from the Spaniard, the Italian, and the Frenchman? Is the future for the Teuton, the Scandinavian, the Saxon, and the Sclave? And are the Latin nations sinking into the condition in which we now see their predecessors in imperial power — into the condition of Phœnicia, of Egypt, and of Greece? Or will they become revivified by the new stimulus of liberty; by the abandonment of old enthralments, the shaking off of absolute kingship, and the perhaps still more binding despotism of priestcraft; will they be leavened by democracy, regain their savor by the salt of republicanism?

Certain it is that for a long time the Latin races have been declining and waning under the old condition of things; that, had Bomba reigns in Italy, rules of later Ferdinands and Isabellas in Spain, and Bourbon incubi in France, continued, this descent would have gone on. No doubt, too, this descent has been, to the observer's eye, arrested by the new life infused by revolution. France is surely to-day better, stronger, more self-contained, for the young Republic which has so completely altered the political aspect of things during the last seven years. Will this improvement continue — is it permanent and become organic? Or is it but a temporary delay in the general downward course of the brilliant and thrifty Gallic race?

Equally apparent is it that Italy, united and become constitutional, refreshed by the wise, temperate, reasonable rule of Victor Emmanuel, whose successor has had the sober sense to follow in his father's footsteps, is a better, and in many senses a more prosperous country than it was, or could possibly have been, under Bomba and the Austrians and the petty Dukes. But Italy, too, is on trial, like the French. In the long stretch of particular events and special

phases in the progress of a nation, the constitu-
tionalism, the reign of the house of Savoy, even
the unity of Italy, may be but bright incidents,
to be followed by anarchy and perhaps reim-
posed tyranny of kings and priests.

Of these Latin races, the Spanish are behind
their brother heirs to the legacy of the Roman
conquerors of Europe. Spain seems to have
been marked out for the very worst scourges
which the ingenuity of political and priestly
tyrants could devise. It has not been split up,
like Italy, into fragments, each fragment the victim of a different despot. It has not been so
frightfully desolated by hotly raging wars and
invasions humiliating the people in the dust, as
France. Perhaps Spain to-day would be better
off had she passed through these fiery furnaces.
She has suffered ills perhaps even yet more
far-reaching in their results, penetrating more
deeply, leaving graver and more obstinate moral
and political disease. It would probably have
seemed to a thoughtful student, twenty-five years
ago, as if nothing good *could* come out of Spain.
Such a student would have been puzzled to
recognize, under the dismal, gloomy, brazen,
corrupt reign of Isabella, the Spain which, within

the period of a single century, between 1540 and
1640, had displayed warrior sovereigns like
Charles the Fifth and Philip the Second, soldiers
like Alva, conquerors like Pizarro, painters like
Velasquez and Murillo, churchmen like Loyola,
and writers like Cervantes and Calderon de la
Barca. Indeed from the time of Calderon, who
died in 1687, down to very recent years, Spanish
history, as far as either national glory or intellectual activity is concerned, presents an almost
uniformly dreary blank. Who can name a single
Spanish statesman of the rank of Ximenes, or
any Spanish writer or painter of any extended
reputation at all, who lived and labored in the
eighteenth century? Italy had at least Alfieri.
France teemed with keen, inquiring, brilliant
minds. But of Spanish intellectual effort, of any
such thing as searching politico-philosophic activity, it would be hard to find a definite stamp
between the accession of Philip the Fifth and
the deposition of Isabella the Second. The intellectual torpor seemed absolute; and out of a
soil so drearily barren, how could we expect any
excellent intellectual fruit to grow and thrive?

Yet it is true that, within the past ten years,
signs that eloquence, philosophy, culture, and

political wisdom have rather been dormant than extinct in Spain, have here and there pretty plainly shown themselves. Certain Spanish figures have appeared, who have astonished men by their attitude, dignity, talent and sound sense. And when such figures do appear in a nation's career, and make themselves seen, heard, listened to and respected, all hope of that nation cannot be lost. That the art of eloquence still survives in Spain, that enlightenment in its very highest intellectual form is still a possibility there, that great principles of government and liberty may even yet find nourishment in its so long sterile soil, may be seen in the character and career of Emilio Castelar.

It is curious and somewhat mysterious how this professor of history, young, handsome, and with a romantic name, came forth from the cloistral quiet of the University of Madrid, to become at one time a stormy petrel of street revolt, at another a fervidly eloquent orator in the Cortes, and again the rather impracticable President of a short-lived republic. He burst as suddenly into fame, as far as the trans-Pyrenean world was concerned, as Gambetta had done at Paris; and all at once the world was shown that

Spain was still capable of producing genius, learning, and political foresight.

Castelar was born at Alicante, of a good but not noble family, in 1832. At forty-one he held the chief executive power of Spain, and was for a short time its absolute dictator. Now, at forty-seven, he has still, undoubtedly, a brilliant career before him. The records of his earlier years, before he became known as the undaunted chief of the republicans, are scant, and of no large interest. He went up to the University from Alicante in his teens; was soon known as one of the most enthusiastic of its students; assumed and kept the head of his various classes; betrayed a special taste for history and political philosophy; and on graduation was appointed an instructor. But long before this he had plainly declared the principles accepted by his reason, which the ripening of his mind and his somewhat rough experience in life seem only to have confirmed. At the age of sixteen he harangued a Madrid mob with such surprising power of speech that he became an object of dread to the government itself. In that harangue he avowed extreme republican opinions; his appeal to the people was hotly revolutionary. In-

deed, Castelar has since declared, " I have been
a conspirator from boyhood." Before his beard
was grown he was consorting with insurgents,
attending secret conclaves held in dark by-
streets, writing fiery proclamations to be posted
in the dead of night on the walls of Madrid, and
holding correspondence with republicans of note
in other lands. But conspiracy in Spain is not
only permanently fashionable; it does not there
seem in the least to affect a man's standing, or
to taint his personal honor. Every Spanish
statesman, of whatever party, has been a conspirator at some time or other. When O'Donnell was in power, Espartero conspired; when
Espartero was in power, Narvaez conspired.
Serrano and Prim conspired against the throne;
Figueras against Serrano and Prim. Royal blood
is infected with this mania. The Duke of Montpensier has been a life-long conspirator; and
Don Carlos has never ceased either plotting or
rebelling.

In spite of Castelar's republican zeal, he was
in early manhood appointed professor of history in the University. He was the best man
in Spain, perhaps in Europe, to fill that chair;
but it is strange how it came to pass that he was

allowed to assume it. The government of Isabella was singularly capricious in its tolerance and its tyranny. Towards some classes, it was as bitterly despotic as were the Philips; but it saw, apparently without protest, the election of a learned rebel to the chair of history. The new professor by no means ceased from plotting after entering upon his duties. He taught republicanism and revolution in his very class-room. He gathered about him the ardent youths of the University, and saturated their receptive minds with the idea and principle of political liberty. He told them, with an accuracy of fact and a correctness of interpretation which in a Spaniard was nothing less than marvellous, the story of the rise and progress of the free republic of the United States; and pointed to it and its constitution as the model which he aspired to have Spain adopt. He argued in favor of the abolition of slavery, of a confederation of Spanish provinces, abolition of the tie between Church and State, universal suffrage, free education. All this was going on under the very eyes of Isabella's ministers, and it was not stopped. The professor was not content to show the faith that was in him by mere words alone.

He was still consorting with conspirators, the central spirit of midnight cabals. Then came a day of revolt in the streets of Madrid; and in the midst of the mob appeared the figure of the professor, as little professorial in speech and action as possible; now a fervid orator, pouring out language of incendiary eloquence, and leading his hot-headed followers boldly to barricade and barracks. We should be somewhat astonished to hear of the dean of Christ Church, Oxford, or the professor of moral philosophy at Cambridge, leading a London mob to an attack on Buckingham Palace. It evidently did not appear strange, however, to the Madrid populace, to see the university expounder of history in full insurrection. Marshal Serrano speedily put down this rising, which was the forerunner of that later rising which he himself successfully led. Castelar was taken prisoner and thrown into prison. His offence, however, was a very commonplace and usual one. He was not very strictly guarded, though he was condemned to death. By the aid of friendly rebels outside, he soon, with little difficulty, escaped. He went to Geneva and thence to Paris, at both of which places he was warmly received by fellow-exiles. Meanwhile, he kept a keen watch on events in Spain; he guessed what was coming. The time of waiting did not hang heavily on his hands, for he had a more than facile pen. Spain has not produced in modern times a more brilliant, lucid and prolific writer. He had already served a long apprenticeship in journalism. While still quietly pursuing his professorial duties, he had been a frequent contributor to no less than four Spanish newspapers, in all of which he luminously and vigorously argued for the republican cause. Now, at Paris, he wrote for English and French periodicals, besides sending heavy rolls of manuscript to Madrid.

At the first forewarning sound of the revolution of 1868, Castelar hurried back to his native land. He was sorely needed by his eager republican countrymen, and he instantly responded to their call. He hoped that Serrano, Prim, and Topete might do the work of democracy. Isabella's rule had become insufferable in its corruption, degradation and imbecility, even for those stout old soldiers and courtiers. At all events, in the hurly-burly of civil war, the opportunity to attempt the establishment of a republic must not be lost. Castelar was welcomed home

with the wildest enthusiasm, and with Orense and
Figueras at once took the lead of a republican
movement. But the trio of old soldiers were, at
the time, too much for these radicals. They had
the army and navy with them, while Castelar had
with him only the mob of Madrid, Barcelona and
a few other large towns; and Madrid is not to
Spain what Paris is to France. Prim became
dictator, with the understanding that he was to
keep the seat of power warm until a sovereign of
the pliant sort could be hunted up and got ready
to take it. But at the same time the republican
chiefs were chosen to seats in the new Cortes.
Castelar sought election as deputy for his native
town, Alicante, but was defeated by priestly
influence. While urging his claims at Alicante,
with pardonable pride, he suddenly exclaimed,
" My fellow-citizens, my name is sculptured from
the Alps to the Andes ! " His rejection there
did not exclude him from the Cortes, for he
was soon after chosen as one of the representatives of the capital.

It was during that memorable first session of
the revolutionary legislature that Castelar appeared in his full stature as a statesman and as
an orator. It was one thing to fire a mob with

burning appeals; another to discuss grave measures, to aid in shaping a new constitution, and
to produce a practical effect upon a sober assemblage composed at once of the best minds
and of the most inveterate prejudices of Spain.
Yet there was no old royalist *hidalgo* so dull and
obstinate as not to recognize at once the splendor of his eloquence, rich with the ripest and
aptest illustrations drawn from vast and well-
digested lore, or the broad reach of his political
ideas, which comprehended lessons drawn from
the experience of every race, ancient and modern. With a small minority of republican colleagues to sustain him by their votes, Castelar
was yet a formidable power in the constituent
Cortes. Prim, with all his force of brevity and
directness, with all his strong sense and practical
knowledge of politics, found out very early that
he was no match for Castelar in debate ; and the
priest orators of the Cortes, the best, as a rule,
that it contained, soon evidently shrank from
crossing rhetorical lances with him. His mission in this Cortes was plain — to get the constitution as near the republican form and spirit
as possible, and to educate Spaniards to a faith
in, and appreciation of, republican institutions.

As each grave question came up, Castelar was
found ready to meet it with a solution deduced
from his own political creed. His first action
was to insist that that life-long royal conspirator,
the Duke of Montpensier, should be removed
from the command-in-chief of the army. Topete,
one of the trio of successful revolutionists, was
known to favor Montpensier's elevation to the
vacant throne, in which Prim was serving as a
sort of warming-pan; and it was suspected that
Prim himself was not averse from this *dénoue-
ment*. Failing to attain his purpose, Castelar
next fervidly attacked the proposal that monarchy was the form of government desired by
the nation. Here he had the enemy in the open
field, and he assailed them along the whole line.
Nothing could exceed the courage, the vigor,
the exhaustive illustration, the infectious warmth
with which he now spoke. The speeches which
he delivered at that critical moment are still
clearly remembered and often quoted by Spaniards. He painted in the most vivid colors the
blight which monarchy had already spread over
the land; the abasement which Spain, under the
Bourbons, had long ago reached, and in which
she still remained. "*Señores,*" he exclaimed in

tones of passionate indignation and sorrow, "look abroad in Spain! We are a vast charnel-house, stretching from the Pyrenees to the Gulf of Cadiz. We have no agriculture, no industry, no trade; that is what your kings have done for us!" Stretching his arm toward Italy, he said, "In Italy, Garibaldi held a crown in his hand at Naples. Instead of destroying it, he gave it to the house of Savoy. But the house on whose head he put a crown, put a bullet into his body at Aspromonte, and a deeper one into his heart at Mentone!"

But Castelar was soon to rise to a yet loftier height of eloquence than that of his speeches against monarchy, inspired as he now was by a yet nobler cause than that of giving a republican form to the future government. This was the cause of religious toleration. The "last ditch" of the old-time power of the Romish priesthood seems to be in Spain. After France had become alienated, and Austria had grown cold, Spain was still fervid in superstition, intolerance, and blind devotion to the Papal crown. The Cortes swarmed with able, and subtle, and tireless bishops and priests. Their whole force and influence were bent upon preserving the traditional proscription of their church and orders. With them they held the fractions of the reactionary parties which had secured a representation in the chamber. The battle between the elements of progress and those of ecclesiastical despotism raged for days. It strained both sides to their utmost desperate exertions. Castelar then had to meet, one after another, the most powerful clerical orators of Spain; and one after another he put them completely to rout.

Prim, who was as liberal as he dared to be, proposed a constitutional clause establishing complete religious toleration for both Spaniards and foreigners; and on this question the whole body of republicans rallied enthusiastically to his side. The clause was assailed by the clerical deputies, who declared that it was inspired by atheists and iconoclasts. This charge brought Castelar promptly to his feet. He launched out in an address which is said to have overwhelmed all sides with literally speechless admiration. Every deputy hung spell-bound on his lips. He drew upon all the vast resources of history to emphasize his plea that religious oppression should be forever abolished from the soil of Spain. In the deepest colors he depicted the crushing and desolating religious oppressions of Philip the Second, and held up degraded, desolated and impoverished Spain before the eyes of his breathless auditors. Then, drawing himself up, and in solemn and trembling tones, he ended with this sublime burst of passionate eloquence: —

"God is great in Sinai; the thunder precedes Him, the lightning attends Him, the light enshrouds Him, the earth trembles, the mountains fall in fragments. But there is a greater God than that. On Calvary, nailed to a cross, wounded, thirsting, dying, He prays, 'Father, forgive my executioners, pardon my persecutors, for they know not what they do!' Great is the religion of power, but greater is the religion of love. Great is the religion of implacable justice, but greater is the religion of pardoning mercy. And I, in the name of that religion — I, in the name of the Gospel — appeal to you, legislators of Spain, to place in the front of your fundamental constitution, liberty, equality, fraternity with all mankind!"

The effect of this rhapsody upon all who heard it is said to have been electric and amazing. The deputies sprang to their feet, as if moved

by a single impulse of irrepressible admiration.
The President left his platform to embrace the
orator. He was nearly smothered by the dem-
onstrations of his friends. The session was suspended spontaneously, without formal motion;
the bishops and canons could not, that day, find
words in which to clothe their opposition.

When, several days after, the discussion was
resumed, Castelar, flushed with his recent triumph, again returned to the plea for religious
liberty. He declared himself still to be a faithful Catholic — "the religion typified by the
marble cross that stretches its holy arms over
the spot most sacred of all the earth to me —
the tomb of my mother!" Then turning to the
benches where the priest-deputies sat, he exclaimed, quoting the words of Jesus concerning
toleration, "Gentlemen, you are at war with the
Head of your church! Were I a priest, I would
pray God, 'bless these legislators, who are enact-
ing on the earth Thy justice and Thy grace!'"

In this struggle Castelar happily formed one
of the majority. Toleration was decreed as an
article of the new constitution, by a vote which,
it is not too much to say, was greatly swelled by
the influence of his splendid eloquence. In so

using it, too, Castelar had much augmented his own political authority. Prim courted and tried to make terms with him. The older republican chiefs willingly admitted him to a full equality with themselves in the councils of the party. A little later, he displayed the wisdom of statesmanship as well as republican ardor. A radical revolt broke out in Madrid. Its chiefs and instigators were his friends. But he used every effort to calm the storm of popular fury, and urged upon the insurgents patience and self-control. Prim was savagely indignant at the revolt, and proposed to suspend liberty and to resort to martial law. Castelar and his colleagues met this threat by another, that if it was carried out they would retire from the Cortes. Prim appealed to him not to do so, and made a further threat. "If we remain in the Cortes," answered Castelar, "it will be from patriotism — not from fear." Prim's motion was carried; Castelar and his friends retired; and he did not for some months reappear in his seat.

The republicans found themselves, for a period, helpless. They could not prevent the election of the Italian prince Amadeus as king; but they remained quiet, for they foresaw that his rule

would soon prove a failure. The sudden abdi-
cation of Amadeus, early in 1873, at last left the
way open to Castelar, Figueras, and Echegeray
to try the experiment of a republic. It was one
of those peaceful revolutions that sometimes take
the whole world by surprise — sudden, bloodless,
and for the time at least, complete. The republic was formally declared in a hitherto monarchical Cortes by a vote of two hundred and fifty-six
to thirty-two. A provisional government was at
once created, and a project for a constituent assembly matured. Figueras, a remarkable type
of character for a Spaniard, grave, pure, puri-
tanical in the soberness and tenacity of his republican faith, a man of fifty, in delicate health,
frank, but too little used to practical politics, was
chosen President of the republic; and Castelar
became his Minister of Foreign Affairs. But
this young government, composed of able and
eloquent but in public affairs inexperienced men,
had infinite difficulties with which to contend.
Spain became a seething vat of conspiracy.
Serrano and Sagasta began to plot; the military
men were jealous and disaffected; the Montpensier party were busy seeking an opportunity
to seize upon power; the Isabellists on one

hand, the Carlists on the other, continually threatened the existence of the new and essentially experimental *régime*. Then again, the ardent republican ministers tried to do too much. Sweeping schemes of reform teemed in their brains, and bloomed into measures at once generous and impracticable. To abolish slavery in Cuba, and gradually throughout the dominion of Spain, and to create in Spain herself a federal government after the pattern of the United States, were only two of the many purposes which Castelar was eager, in the moment of his authority, to carry out. The republic had its hands more than full even to get itself accepted and tolerated, even to get permission to put itself on trial. Unhappily, Castelar — who, from the first, was the controlling genius — aimed to metamorphose Spanish opinion, custom, form, and aspirations in a year's time.

In a few months the strain proved too much, at least for the frail-bodied and, in action, rather timid Figueras. In August, 1873, Castelar exchanged his portfolio for the presidential chair of the new Cortes; and it was but a few weeks later, on the sixth of September, that Figueras resigned, and Castelar was elevated to the presidency of the republic. His first act on assuming the direction of the executive power gave promise of an at least energetic administration. He suddenly dissolved the Cortes, and assumed the dictatorship of Spain. This was done with the honest intent to serve the cause of republican liberty; but how sadly Spanish it was! After all, he could only follow in the track of Prim and O'Donnell. He then tried, by extraordinary measures, to subdue the Cuban insurrection on the one hand, and the Carlist rebellion on the other. But he failed, as the generals would not heartily co-operate with him. Then the dictator was forced to summon a new Cortes into existence. This was opening the jar which let out upon him the giant who was destined to crush him. The Chamber met on the first of January; its first act was to pass a vote of want of confidence in the President; its next, to receive and accept his resignation. Then General Pavia captured the government with his troopers, sent the astonished legislators about their business, gave the dictatorship to Serrano, and the republic had vanished.

It would be unjust to pass a very harsh judgment on Castelar's brief Presidency. He was honest, ardent, full of faith, intensely patriotic, and full of energy. He did not measure at their true magnitude the difficulties that confronted him on every side. He overestimated the intelligence and the political sense of Spaniards. He sadly wanted experience in office. He was betrayed by jealousies and plottings in his own party. He was eager to go too fast. He fell sooner than he might, from excess of zeal; however able and practical, he must, in Spain at that time, have fallen later, if not sooner. The experiment was not a success; but it may be said that perhaps it has left a germ out of which success may some time bud and bloom. Spain is more likely to become a republic from the fact that it has been one.

When the dictatorship of Serrano gave way to the Bourbon restoration in the person of Alfonso, Castelar retired for a while from political life, resigned his professorship in the University, and took up his residence at Geneva. After remaining there a year, however, he returned to Spain, and once more took his seat in the Cortes as the representative of the city of Madrid. This seat he still holds. At the age of forty-eight, Castelar still has doubtless a brilliant career in scholarship and letters, if not in politics, before him. Indeed, while in the midst of the political. hurly-burly, he has never, except at short intervals, allowed his attention to altogether stray from his favorite studies and literary labors. While Minister of Foreign Affairs, many articles from his brilliant pen appeared in English and other periodicals; one in particular on his chief, Figueras, was read with especial admiration in the pages of the *Fortnightly Review.* His range of literary production has been by no means confined to political studies. Besides such works as " Democratic Ideas " and " The Republican Movement in Europe," he has published books on " Popular Legends," " Civilization in the First Five Centuries of Christianity," " Celebrities of the World of Letters," and a most graphic description of " Old Rome and New Italy." It is a matter of special interest to Americans to know how profound and appreciative a study Castelar has made of our institutions. There is something marvellous in the intimacy of his knowledge and the accuracy of his interpretation of them. Without ever having crossed the Atlantic, he seems, by the intuition of sympathetic genius, to have caught their very spirit as successfully as did De Tocqueville himself. Both in his speeches in the Cortes and in the products of his pen, he has constantly referred to the United States as the example he would have Spain set before herself; and many of his most forcible illustrations have been drawn from the same source of political knowledge. Castelar seems to have been especially struck by the guarantees of order and liberty afforded by the federative feature of our government. While in office, he made a bold but futile attempt to introduce it into Spain. He imagined that, with the local peculiarities and dissimilarities to be found among the Basques of the Pyrenees, the Castilians of central Spain, and the Granadans and Andalusians of the South, their veins darkened and heated by a tinge of the Moorish blood, the federative principle, affording at once local self-control and a central bond of union, would be likely to insure the endurance of the young republic. It was a dream which may be realized sometime in the future. What is especially striking is the high enlightenment of Castelar's views and government; the astonishing historic lore he has betrayed, ranging from Russia to North and South America, from Spain to the far Orient, including a profound knowledge of the sources of the Bible, and an easy familiarity with every political system that has prevailed in the world from the most remote to the most recent periods. He has, besides, a memory of which Macaulay might have been jealous, and a power of attention which Sir William Hamilton would scarcely fail to recognize as genius.

As an orator, Castelar probably has in Gambetta his only rival in continental Europe. He has been called " the Wendell Phillips of Spain." Colonel John Hay, who was our Secretary of Legation at Madrid during the brief career of the republic, and who knew Castelar intimately, says of his eloquence: " There is something superhuman in his delivery. His speech is like a torrent in its inconceivable fluency, like a raging fire in its brilliancy of color and terrible energy of passion. His action is most energetic and impassioned. The whole man talks, from his head to his feet." And if he rivals Gambetta in the fluency, the fire and the persuasiveness of his manner, in certain respects — in the richness and fulness of his historical illustrations, in the glowing splendor and inexhaustible resources of his rhetoric, and in the cosmopolitan breadth of his ideas — he certainly surpasses the great French tribune. Some quotations from his speeches in the Cortes have been given; but these can only give an inadequate impression of his oratorical powers. Suffice it to say that he never spoke, even to an audience deadly hostile to his cause, without holding every mind enthralled under his magic spell.

Castelar does not, in his personal appearance, belie the brilliancy of his intellectual or the warmth and nobility of his moral qualities. Colonel Hay thinks that he resembles Shakespeare, as portrayed in marble by a sculptor of the present century. "He reminds you constantly," he says, "of Chantrey's bust of the greatest of the sons of men. The same pure oval outline, the arched eyebrows, the piled-up dome of forehead stretching outward from the eyes, until the glossy black hair, seeing the hopelessness of disputing the field, has retired discouraged to the back of the head." It may be inferred from this that Castelar's personal appearance is prepossessing. Of medium height, or perhaps a little below medium height, his shoulders are broad, his chest is deep, and his bearing of the body is commanding. His face

is a long oval, after the Spanish type; the only
beard worn is a long sweeping mustache, dark,
glossy and evidently carefully cultivated, which
nearly covers the weakest feature of the face —
the mouth. It is not a mouth from which one
infers a very great amount of firmness of character. The complexion is a dark, clear, smooth
olive. The chin shares with the mouth the lack
of strength which we usually expect to see in
the countenance of a man of action — especially
in a revolutionary chief; but it is handsomely
smooth and round. The forehead, while lofty,
is rather narrow, and the eyes are expressively
large, full, and dark, and give its tone to the
whole face. They are the eyes of a poet, an
orator, a man of keen sensibility, a theorizer, a
dreamer of mystical utopianisms. His manner
is simple, dignified, and his gestures are expressive, quick, natural and nervous. When talking, the mobility of his features adds to the eloquence of his words. In attire, Castelar is little
heedful of appearances. His dress is careless,
almost slovenly; and this was at one time a prolific subject of the satire of his enemies.

Castelar's mode of living has always been
simple, modest, economical, after what he con-

ceives to be a republican fashion. Even when
President of the republic, he failed to assume
any of the state which might naturally be supposed to be appropriate to that station. A single
soldier guarded the entrance to the presidential
mansion; the President, who is a bachelor, lived
upon the third floor, in the apartment of his
sister and brother-in-law. Miss Kate Field, in
"Ten Days in Spain," thus describes her visit to
this apartment: —

"On ringing the bell, a man without livery
appeared. Señor Castelar would be disengaged
shortly. Nothing could be plainer than the two
small rooms into which I was ushered. Engrav-
ings of the Spanish masters hung upon the walls.
Besides these, a bronze statuette of Don Quix-
ote, another of Mirabeau, a few books, and an
enormous bouquet, were the sole ornaments of
the apartment."

In private life, Castelar is respected for the
severity of his tastes and correctness of his
habits, and is beloved for the sweetness, the
amiability, the accessibility, and the unaffected
fervor of his nature. His resemblance to Gambetta as an impassioned orator is not greater
than his resemblance to Gambetta as an incor-

ruptible tribune of the people, living (as Gambetta lived down to the period of his assumption of the Presidency of the Chamber of Deputies) in modest lodgings, dressing with almost affected carelessness, and either having or assuming a democratic manner with everybody. On the other hand, Castelar lacks evidently what we should call the "grit" of Gambetta; his immense ability to direct events; his consummate tact as well as vigor in the use of the weapons of practical politics. He is, besides, more of a bookish man than Gambetta; fonder of literature, and a far riper product of long-continued self-culture.

His voice is less often heard in the Cortes than formerly; and it seems doubtful, even should the republic be restored, whether Castelar would be its directing spirit. But he is still, and will always be, the centre of a devoted group of political adherents who love, trust, and follow him. His task would seem rather to educate Spaniards in republicanism than to guide the helm after it has been attained; to illustrate it by his vast learning and his matchless eloquence, rather than to frame its codes and execute its mandates. He by no means despairs of the cause in which he was at one time the prophet,

and at another the martyr; he regards the monarchy as a temporary makeshift and the republic as certain to return in due time. Meanwhile,
his republican preaching through the press, at
the weekly reunions that are held at his house,
and in quiet conferences here and there, goes on
bravely and ceaselessly. Such a man is capable
of leavening a large lump of Spanish ignorance
and prejudice; and it is not unlikely that his
name will live in history as at least the founder
of the republican idea in the so long despot-
ridden and priest-ridden Iberian peninsula.

VI.

VICTOR HUGO.

O N a certain dismal, drizzly afternoon in September, 1870, a large crowd assembled, in
spite of the inclement weather, at the Northern
railway-station in Paris. It was an eager, expect-
ant crowd; mostly in the blouse of the lower
orders, though here and there were well-dressed
men, and men of distinguished appearance and
presence. Paris was at that moment in deep
mourning. Sedan had just been lost; the effort
to bar the German flood of invasion had failed;
and the enemy was now known to be swarming towards the dismayed and anarchy-stricken
capital.

After the crowd had waited till the fine rain
had penetrated to their skins, a long train rolled
into the station. A part of it, however, remained
outside the building when it stopped; and to
this part the crowd hastily huddled. In another
moment a loud, enthusiastic cheer resounded in
the air. Brawny arms were stretched out toward

the platform near one of the cars; hats were waved convulsively; the crowd became a solid, compact mass as near this spot as possible.

An old man, with bare, gray head and flushed face, stood upon the platform. His chest heaved with emotion. He waved his hands nervously towards those who had come to welcome him. He held his head high, as if proud to be so greeted: and waited for the cheers to subside before he opened his mouth to speak.

The venerable face and figure were well worth observing. The remarkable feature of the form was its proud erectness, though sixty-five years of a life full of vicissitude rested upon it. Of medium height, the figure was thick-set and solid; a strong, healthy one, the result of life-long temperance and plenty of physical exercise. The head was round, the forehead high, and arched, and white, the face a broad oval; the hair was cut short and of snowy whiteness, the beard and mustache were also cropped close, gray, and fast whitening. The complexion told a cheerful tale of ruddy health and moderateness of habit; it has been described as that of "a ripe winter apple;" fair and rosy as a child's, and as yet but little wrinkled. The most beautiful feature was

the eye,—large, jet-black, magnificently brilliant,
earnest, with the fire of imagination and genius
burning brightly in it; yet, as he looked down
upon his welcomers, kindly, paternal, moist with
the profoundest emotion. This eye lighted up
the whole face, and made it an irresistibly attractive one. It was not, perhaps, what would be
called a handsome face, but it surely had been,
years ago; it was now a noble, intellectual, be-
nevolent face; that, unquestionably, of a man
above and apart from his fellow-men.

There were gray-heads in the crowd who remembered this man when, just about twenty
years before, he had been driven an exile from
France, to which he now for the first time returned; and they called to mind how, when he
went, his hair had been almost raven-black, and
his face had beamed with all the glories of the
intellectual beauty of younger manhood. He
had greatly changed; but age had ennobled
him, and made him look far grander than before.

Strange words — strangely eloquent and powerful, and altogether surprising — were those
which, when his clear, warm voice could be
heard, greeted the ears of his hearers. He
plunged into a harangue in which pathos, imagi-

nation, poetry, and extravagance of language, were grotesquely blended. He spoke of France as the focus of civilization, and of Paris as the intellectual metropolis of the globe. In splendid diction, with sentences bejewelled with epigram and studded with simile, he sounded all the glories of his native land. He told his auditors that the Germans would never dare to lay their vandal hands upon sacred Paris; that as she sat there, peerless amid her hills, her very aspect would awe the intruder into hasty retreat. Then, stretching forth his arms in the drizzling rain in the direction whence the German armies were approaching the capital, he addressed to them an appeal, which at one moment we are prone to think of as sublime, and in the next as ludicrous. He besought the German hosts to dethrone their kings, to desert their generals, to lay down their arms, to hasten to the embrace of their French brethren, and, with them, to declare "the universal republic!"

The life of this greatest of all French romancers — for what French novel-writer, living or dead, could match any one of his own works with "Les Miserables"? — has been itself a romance. One shrinks from attempting to portray that

meteor-like career, — the splendor of its triumphs, the depth of its sorrows, its unexpected
dénoucments, its displays of passion, of fancy, of
profound thought, of a charity and humane
yearnings that have embraced all mankind, its
creations of literary schools, and its defiances of
autocratic power; and still less hopeful is the
task of justly weighing and describing the quality
and characteristics of this genius, which has
moved and startled men for more than fifty years,
and the resources of which are apparently far
from being even yet exhausted.

This ardent republican is the son of a Bona-
partist general and of a Legitimist mother, and
the grandson of an old noble who was guillotined
by Robespierre. Born when the power of Napoleon was at its height, he was reared amid the
thrilling and troublous events which marked
Napoleon's decline and fall. He is, moreover,
of noble blood; for General Hugo, his father,
dated his nobility two centuries back, and his
mother was patrician enough to have joined in
the royalist conspiracy of La Vendée. Victor
Hugo's childhood was passed amid scenes well
fitted to nurture the soul of a poet. That poverty which he has portrayed so often and with

such tender eloquence, he himself never suffered. His beauty and brightness as a child were the theme of all who saw him. Before he had reached his eighth year he had seen more of the great world than most men during their lives. His first recollections brought before his mind's eye the new-fangled and showy court of the great Napoleon. At five, he found himself amid the Calabrian mountains, where his father was busy trapping the famous brigand, Fra Diavolo. He travelled in Italy, studied in a convent, learned to read the Latin historians precociously soon; again lived in Spain, and took in all that he saw and learned with keen eye and rapid mind. These early associations made a gentleman, and a scholar, and a poet of Victor Hugo; and he has carried the polish of intellectual refinement and the grace of the old-time manner then learned, through revolution, riot, the storms of the tribune, and his apostolate of the rights of the people.

Victor Hugo published poetry worth reading and remembering at ten years of age. Four years later he produced a tragedy; at fifteen he wrote an essay for the prize of the Academy, which was only withheld from him because the

Academicians could not believe that such a strip-
ling composed it.   Then began that marvellous
literary career which has continued to amaze
mankind for more than half a century.   A mere
record of Victor Hugo's literary triumphs would
go far to exhaust the space at my disposal.   He
was a distinguished man at twenty, the favorite
poet of the Bourbon Restoration, the master of
the revels at the games of Toulouse, christened
by Chateaubriand "the sublime child," granted
a pension by the king, and admired throughout
Paris for his noble grace and bearing and his
brilliant personal beauty.   It then seemed as if
Victor Hugo was destined to become another
Racine; an elegant ornament of courts, a starred
noble, perhaps a staid politician, and a prospec-
tive, polite and loyal minister of fine arts.   His
imagination, now crystallizing into beautiful and
vigorous forms, decorated the Bourbon throne
with floral crowns and wreaths of poesy such as
had never before adorned it.   He endowed the
dull and narrow-souled Charles X. with knightly
qualities and heroism such as his genius alone
could have lifted and protected from the laughter of the world.   Royal mouths spoke of him as
Orpheus and Apollo in one.   But at that time

no one suspected in the young bard, who had already drunk in the full meaning of Lamartine's "Meditations," other thoughts or aspirations than those inspired by a blind idolatry of thrones.

To a mind at once so clear, so susceptible, and so sensitive as that of Victor Hugo, the awakening to the consciousness that the idols of his childhood and youth were coarse and common clay, must have been a terrible one. His happiness and his ambition rested in his thoughts; and to find that he had wasted the rich gold of his fancy upon that which was unworthy, seems to have gradually transformed him. Victor Hugo for the first time became a politician when his fair dreams of royal honor and beneficence were rudely dispelled, and his eyes were opened to a suffering people struggling beneath the throne. The young poet then betrayed the nobility of his nature; its courage, its sincerity, and its deep-feeling humanity. He boldly cast his false gods behind him. He approached the political descendants of those who had guillotined his grandsire; of those whom his revered mother, at the risk of her very life, had conspired to overthrow. The glamour of the Napoleonic legend faded and shrivelled before his eyes; the divinity

that had seemed to him to hedge kings, deserted
the throne, and hovered now above the people.
The new thoughts did not come upon him all at
once; he was not converted, like Paul, in a blind-
ing flash of light. His muse at first became dumb.
There were no more magnificent pæans sung to
the surpassing excellence of Bourbon royalty.
The crowding thoughts were stemmed and pent
up. This teeming, unresting mind was for a time
congested with unuttered thoughts and imagin-
ings. It must be confessed, too, that praise was
sweet to him, and that his silence was freezing
the praise that lingered on high-born lips, ready
to lavish itself when he should sing again.

Then he cut adrift from the past. The word
went forth that the pet poet of the Restoration
was no longer its flatterer and laureate. He
turned from the composition of sycophantic odes
to that of virile and fiery romances. He founded
a liberal club. He began to talk fervidly of the
rights of the people. He established and edited
a paper devoted to literary and political reform;
and now that he was fairly abroad on the new
road, he gave bold battle to other things that
were ancient besides the monarchy. The false
gods of the throne were not the only ones

against whom he hurled the whole force of his eloquence and genius. He became the apostle of a new literature. He braved the big-wigs of the Academy itself; revolted from classic perfection of form, and championed the cause of pure and great ideas; he sought to pull down Aristotle from his pedestal, and Racine from his; he praised Voltaire; he locked arms with Lamartine; and in his tragedy of " Cromwell," given to the world when he was twenty-five, laid the corner-stone of that romanticism which has become the Parthenon of French literature. No one can, probably, conceive of the intensity of the conflict which then raged between the old and new literary schools, who did not live in its midst; its issue we know, for the triumph of Hugo and Lamartine, if slow, has been complete.

It would seem as if this struggle, and with it the full awakening to a new intellectual life, served to develop powers in Victor Hugo's mind which, with all his reputation and promise, had hitherto been unsuspected. For it was in the very last years of the reign of Charles X., that he produced the dramas which at once placed him above every dramatist of his time, and which contained the revolutionary ideas which he has since only elaborated. "Marion de l'Orme" aroused the terror of the palace, of the Academy, of the patrician classes, of the dramatic censorship. Had it been only revolutionary and commonplace, it might have been ignored with contempt; but it was literary genius flourishing the sword of revolution. Its fiery utterances went straight to the heart and the reason of the people. It was more powerful than Manuel in the Chamber, Royer-Collard at the Sorbonne, or Thiers in the sanctum. It appealed to the popular heart in its recreations. Its performance was forbidden. Then came "Hernani," which was allowed. This leniency was as fatal as the former intolerance had been. "Hernani" inspired a riot on the very eve of Charles's downfall; Victor Hugo was vindicated by the fists of the mob. In his hands the theatre became an engine of revolution quite as effective as the eloquence of the tribune or the power of the press; and in the alliance which effected the final expulsion of the Bourbons, we must reckon the drama, as used by him, as not the least formidable confederate.

His dramas and poems had made him a political as well as a literary figure. So far, however,

was he from the ultimate goal of republican
faith, when the revolution of 1830 took place,
that he seems for the moment to have regretted
the Bourbon downfall. It was at this period that
he produced the first of his great works of enduring fiction, — " Notre Dame de Paris ; " and it is
scarcely an exaggeration to say that up to that
time, no romance written by a French pen had
so stirred the feeling of the masses. Almost for
the first time, we find in " Notre Dame" that
profound and tender sympathy for, and commis-
eration with, the unfortunate, which was in the
process of years to make Victor Hugo, above all
writers, the champion of poverty and humble
virtue. Nor could the reader of " Notre Dame"
fail to discover, in many of its brilliant passages,
the germ of that belief in the brotherhood and
the equality of men, which became the central
idea of Victor Hugo's political creed. Scorn
of kingship, contempt of hereditary privilege,
fiery indignation at the oppressions of the great,
burst forth in its pages, here and there, seemingly almost against the writer's will.

But two years had not elapsed of the reign of
the citizen king, before Victor Hugo again
assailed palace and crown through the avenue of

the drama. Rejected though this no longer questioned genius had been by the Academy, regarded still in polite society as a brilliant but erratic visionary, not yet accepted by the tribunes of the people as one of themselves, as yet more conservative in politics than Thiers or Lamartine, more radical in literature than Royer-Collard or Béranger, Victor Hugo had nevertheless made his power felt over the hearts and imaginations of the masses. "Le Roi s'Amuse" —a thunderbolt of satire and ridicule aimed at the uselessness and caprices of kingship — raised such an uproar even in a "bourgeois" reign, as to terrify Louis Philippe and his ministers, and to cause it to be suppressed by official decree. This seemed a violation of that popular liberty which the revolution had been supposed to secure; but it was also so much the more an unwilling tribute to Victor Hugo's genius. He now became a popular idol; and if, at that moment, he had chosen to leave the field of literature for that of politics, he might have taken his place among the chiefs of the popular party. At the age of thirty, however, with the consciousness of his past triumphs and his ripening genius to inspire him, literature was still too beloved a mistress to quit. The decade between 1832 and 1842 was the most fruitful in his whole life in amount and quality of literary production. He did not in that period reach the very summit of intellectual achievement; that was to be attained when, twenty years later, the incomparable "Les Miserables" was read by a wondering world. But it was between 1832 and 1842 that appeared "Lucretia Borgia," "Marie Stuart," and "Ruy Blas," three magnificent historical dramas which still hold the stage, and have won triumphs in every civilized country; that his masterly "Study of Mirabeau," his "Literature and Philosophy," "Songs of Twilight," the bold martial poem of "The Rhine," "Inner Voices," and "Angels," were written and published. It is not too much to say that at the end of this period, Victor Hugo had attained a degree of literary renown far eclipsing that of Chateaubriand, Lamartine, or Balzac, and only surpassed in the previous century by Voltaire.

It has been said of the contrast between the greatest Greek and the greatest mediæval Italian sculptor, that while Phidias executed serene gods, Michael Angelo portrayed suffering heroes. As one compares the works of Victor

Hugo — those already mentioned — with the performances of the preceding French classics, a similar contrast suggests itself. The revolt which Victor Hugo began at twenty against the formality, the correctness, the rule and measure-governed style of Racine, Corneille, and their schools, he carried on persistently and hotly throughout his literary career. In twenty years he had so far established romanticism as the vital principle of a virile and enduring literature, that scholarly France was very evenly divided between it and the older school; and in 1841 romanticism achieved a victory and unequivocal testimony to its influence, by the admission of Victor Hugo, at last, into the august circle of the French Academy. Four years later a very different and much more singular honor was conferred upon him. Louis Philippe created him a senator of France; but Victor Hugo, though he was well fitted to play a conspicuous part as an academician, was quite out of place among the formal and prosy pundits who then composed the upper house; and his appearances as a "senator" were few and rare. No one as yet suspected that Victor Hugo was capable of high political eloquence; but this was soon to be proven beyond all cavil.

The revolution of 1848 came to stir every
Frenchman with patriotic instincts to the most
anxious thought and earnest endeavor in behalf
of his country. Victor Hugo seems to have
hesitated now for the last time between the influences of his childhood and the convictions of
his ripened intellect. At first he thought of re-
sisting the revolution. When it had become an
accomplished fact, he entered the Constituent
Assembly to cast the weight of his fame and influence in the moderate scale. He feared the
return of the Terror, and shrank from the pros-
pect of Jacobin rule. It is a curious fact that in
those days he sat near Louis Napoleon Bonaparte in the Chamber, and more often voted with
him than on the other side. He was democratic
and republican, but looked askance at the Mountain. Events soon rapidly changed his view of
the political course he should pursue. He was
alarmed at the election of Bonaparte to the
presidency, and already foresaw the shadow of
the Empire lowering over France. In the Legislative Assembly, which succeeded the Constituent, and in which Victor Hugo sat as one of
the representatives of Paris, he finally took his
stand as a champion of popular liberty and

equality, and from that hour to this he has never once swerved from that creed.

And now, at the age of forty-eight, Victor Hugo proved himself a brilliant orator. It was impossible for him to espouse such a cause as this, which fired his imagination and satisfied his intellect, without plunging into it with all the glowing and intense fervor of his nature. He was never a judge, but always a vehement partisan. Of a physical type and presence which filled and attracted the eye, with raven-black hair, a "great, curious eye," an erect, defiant form, a manner absorbingly intent and earnest, a clear, high voice, with every tone and every movement full of passion; and, added to these traits, with pre-eminent renown as a poet and dramatist; it is no wonder that Victor Hugo commanded spell-bound attention. His delivery was tempestuous, rapid, flashing, and, it must be said, often arrogant; he hesitated at no violence or extravagance of language; he did not spare even the most illustrious of his antagonists; he exhausted the resources of a vocabulary overflowing with epithets upon those whom he assailed; with scorn and withering contempt, with denunciations white-hot and scorching, with

ridicule that hissed and seethed, as, like molten
lava, he poured it out upon the objects of his
hostility, he battled for the cause he had wedded
and was intent on bringing to realization. Those
who heard his almost daily forensic conflicts
with Montalembert, a foeman worthy of his
steel, and one who had the advantage of him at
least in temper and logic, speak of those scenes
as scenes never to be forgotten; and those who
sat well-nigh paralyzed, as he hurled his anathe-
mas upon the faithless President of the republic, who was subjecting that republic to a slow
process of assassination, declare that they can
still hear the strident voice and the relentless
words ringing in their ears. Enough has been
said of the character of Victor Hugo's political
temperament and eloquence to show why he
could never be a statesman or a practical politician. It provokes a smile to think of this vehement and extravagant genius framing a formal
code, or leading, by patience and tact, a party
to victory. He was, evidently, an apostle and
preacher of republicanism, and not a law-maker.
He dealt with abstract ideas; sublime ones, indeed, but ideas which could scarcely be so codi-
fied as to govern well the Frenchmen of 1850.

He could see whither poor worried France was
drifting, and the traitor hand preparing the
death-blow for the republic; declamation could
not hold France back, or the traitor hand; yet,
unfortunately, declamation was all that this
proud patriot knew how to do. The greatest
and noblest of the romanticists was in politics
a visionary; and his eloquence, glowing, ardent,
fierce, tremendous in bitterness, scorn and ridicule as it was, could avail nothing, unless it were
to rouse more practical minds from their torpor,
and to inflame the popular mind to revolt against
oppression. The ample proof that Victor Hugo,
brilliant as an orator, vehement as a partisan,
and absorbingly zealous as a patriot, was really
out of place as a politician, lies in his utter help-
lessness at the supreme moment when the
catastrophe which he had long foreseen — the
coup d'état — occurred. That his eloquence had
power and danger in it, however, was abundantly
confessed by the usurper; one of whose first
acts was to banish the brightest literary light of
France from her soil. Then came the long exile
in Jersey, Guernsey, and Brussels; the scornful
rejection of amnesties offered and even urged;
the terrific onslaught upon the Emperor in

"Napoleon the Little;" and there turn of Victor Hugo, fortunately for the world and for his fame, to literary labors. It was during his exile of nineteen years that he wrote "Les Châtiments," a poem of which, as has been well said, "every line breathes living fire, and branded his enemy with indelible disgrace;" that he produced those profound and unsurpassingly pathetic reflections, "Les Contemplations;" that he wrought·out that masterpiece of his genius, "Les Miserables;" and that he betrayed many other evidences of his versatility as well as of his feeling and fancy.

It behooves the student of Victor Hugo's works, no matter how appreciative and loving, to speak cautiously and with measured words of his splendid genius; for there is that in his noblest work which so dazzles and enthralls that the reader is most easily thrown off the balance of his judgment. One is tempted to declare that the entire philosophy and practical teaching of the Christian religion lie between the covers of "Les Miserables;" that not even in Shakespeare is there such deep penetration into human character; that in the chapter on "the Dissection of a Soul," the profoundest depth of spiritual

probing has been reached; that the pathos and
the passion, the minute shades of character, the
marvellous humanity, the all-embracing sympathy, the dramatic power, the superb description, to be found in that romance, have never
before been combined within a single book.
Even the staid Blackwood reviewer is lured from
judicial measure of language when he comes to
speak of "Les Miserables" and "Nôtre Dame."
He says that "they dwarf everything that can
be put by their side;" that there is nothing in
modern literature "which would not look pale
in their presence;" and that "there is no
Frenchman who can be so much as thought of
in any possible aspect of rivalry" with Victor
Hugo. Once the laureate of thrones, in the pas-
sage of years and the process of intellectual
growth he became of all men the literary tribune
of poverty and misfortune. Every subject that
he handles, too, completely possesses him.
Even in his most extravagant passages — and
there are many which to most readers seem to
be enthusiasm gone clean mad — there is apparently no studying for mere effect. Of all things,
Victor Hugo is inartificial. It is not the mere
art of a skilled writer that is observed; this

quality is there, it is true, for without it the
splendid dramatic effects, the surprises, situations, and *dénouements*, the rapid and brilliant
transitions from scorn to pathos, from pathos to
sunny merriment, and from joy to the most sombre tragedy, could not have been wrought out to
such artistic perfection. There is, however,
within and behind, the real and sacred fire of
genius; a harmonious union of imagination and
enthusiasm and dead-in-earnestness. As one
recalls one after another of Victor Hugo's productions, he is tempted to think that love is the
key-note of his soul. He loves France with a
fervor more than patriotic; he almost worships
the grandeur of Paris; he fondly loves nature,
and all things beautiful within it; his mighty
heart reaches forth and embraces mankind;
above all, his tenderest affection is lavished, in
glowing words that fire with like feeling every
other heart that is not dead, with the choicest
flowers of his fancy, the brightest gems of his
intellectual wealth, and the most far-sought
phrases of affection his language affords, upon
the down-trodden and the stricken, the victims
of man's injustice, the desperate hunted ones of
society.

And this quality of great love that appears in his writings, is also the noblest personal quality of the man himself. Between him and the members of his family there has always been the most ardent and devoted affection. There is not an author living sharper at a trade with the publishers; he exacts his due to the uttermost centime. And his due received, it is lavished with bounteous hand right and left, to relieve suffering, to scatter joy, to comfort the lowly, to confer pleasure. All exiles were welcomed to his exiled home at Guernsey with open arms and to a bounteous table. The unfortunate of all lands were his guests and his pensioners. After the fall of the Commune, when Victor Hugo had retired to Brussels, he filled his house there with Communist refugees; and this at the risk not only of his property, but his life. His enthusiastic affection for children is betrayed alike in his works and in his daily acts. There are no more exquisitely beautiful passages in his romances than those in which he describes childhood. There is a caress in every tone, and a benediction in every touch. "The babes," says the reviewer already quoted, "are as distinct as the heroes, every pearly curve of them tender

and sweet as rose-leaves, yet complete creatures,
even in the most delicious softness of execution."
With what loving tenderness does he follow the
growth from childhood to loveliest girlhood, and
noble womanhood, of Cosette! How you can
see his heart wrapt up in this gentle creature,
and almost feel it bound with pleasure when he
returns, from lurid scenes and dreary wicked-
ness, to attend her in another step of her career!
The wrongs done to children make his heart
bleed, and force from him groans of anguish and
agony. "The Man who Laughs" is judged by
the world his least attractive and least creditable
work of fiction; and truly its wild extravagance,
its historical inaccuracies, its imagination gone
to seed, its endless detail, its riot of words and
ideas, render it a not pleasant book, even to his
most zealous admirers. But in "The Man who
Laughs" is the most terrible indictment against
the cruelty of the great and rich that ever was
drawn; and to intensify the enormity of the
selfish barbarism of the class at which he aimed,
he reproduced a most awful example in the person of a bright and tender-hearted child, made
hideous for life for courts and crowds to jeer at.
To the cursory reader, Gwynplaine, "the man

who laughs," is a hideously romantic hero. To those of deeper insight, he is the terrible symbol of the people, whose souls have been mutilated by kings and laws, so that they laugh forever at their own appalling debasement.

It is pleasant to think that the green old age of this master-spirit of literature, this man who is renowned alike as a poet, a novelist, a dramatist, a philosopher, an editor, and an orator, who has worked so splendidly in the cause of the lowly, who has given forth ideas that will surely live, who has uttered truths which must make men better as they spread, and who has shown in his own noble, unselfish, fruitful life, what good things are temperance, benevolence, and self-sacrifice, — it is pleasant to think that his green old age is being passed in the Paris he so dearly loves, and amid the scenes of all his triumphs; that he may contemplate, with serene delight, the founding of a French republic likely to endure, and may himself sit as a life senator of France among its grave councillors. Victor Hugo has never affected the roughness of life and dress, and vulgar familiarity of manner, by which the demagogue sometimes seeks to gain favor with the multitude. He has always lived like a gentleman and a scholar. His house has always been the centre of elegant literary re-unions; his chosen companions have been men of culture and intellect. His modest though cosily garnished house in the Rue Clichy has become, since the return of the great exile, the centre of frequent political and literary recep-tions, at which the first minds in France have gathered to discuss measures and books. Thrice in three years the shadow of death fell upon his house, depriving him of a faithful and be-loved wife, and two sons on whose future he had rested the most sanguine hopes. These great griefs passed, and left the grand old man sadly serene; for he believes in a future life with all his soul, and knows that ere long his own sum-mons must come to rejoin them. No one can approach him without being irresistibly attracted by his beneficent face, his big, kindly glowing eyes, his cordial, almost affectionate warmth of greeting. To every one alike he is approach-able, genial and talkative. As his sympathies reach down to the humblest, so his bearing with all men is outwardly fraternal. What he is in his books, he is in his daily walks; and one has only to read them, to derive an excellent idea of his conversation. It is sparkling, epigrammatic, flowing, full of warmth and feeling, accompanied by expressive action of the features and the hands. He is ready and glad to talk about everything, and amazes by the extent of his erudition, especially in common things. He is easily aroused to a long and brilliant monologue by the introduction of a subject that especially interests him. He never tires of declaiming — for it is declamation — about the hopeful outlook for the republic; about the enormity of the *coup d'état* ; about the necessity of abolishing, by the spread of knowledge, all crime, war, and poverty. His ideas naturally take poetic and grandiose forms as he warms to his theme. He quotes freely from his own works, with graceful apology; and there is throughout an air of what would be called vanity in a lesser man, but which in him is warranted by the consciousness of his pre-eminent fame, and of the reverent admiration of all the world.

In certain respects Victor Hugo has been compared to Thomas Carlyle; and it is hard to think of any other British writer with whom such a comparison could be possible. Carlyle and Hugo, however, have the same panoramic pic-

turcsqueness of delineation, the same poetic insight into events and character, the same complete and powerful method of portraiture, the
same scorn of sham, pretence and privilege, and
the same feverish aspirations for a better world.
But Victor Hugo, as he has grown old, has
grown too in his faith in men; his sympathies
for the oppressed and outcast, his tenderness for
the individual, have broadened and deepened.
But age has made of Carlyle a scoffing cynic,
a disbeliever in human excellence lying beneath
ignorance and poverty, and a fierce advocate of
hero-worship and what he calls beneficent despotism. His beliefs — what few are left to him —
wander in a maze of bewilderment, and refuse to
be defined. Victor Hugo may not be a Catholic;
he may ridicule the stories the priests tell the
people as "old wives' fables;" he may thunder
against the spiritual tyranny of prelates and the
exactions of the clergy; but he who wrote "Les
Miserables" can scarcely be otherwise than a
devoutly-believing Christian. And in this Victor
Hugo rises a long degree higher than almost
every other intellectual Frenchman of his time.

On one occasion, when Victor Hugo was
charged with being an apostate, he replied with

not less truth than vanity, "They call me an
apostate; I believe myself to be an apostle."
This seems accurately to define his place, alike
in letters and in politics. He has been the
apostle, truly, of a new, vital, vigorous, soulful
literature, which is moral, elevating, fervid,
imaginative, moving, and full of inspiration. He
has been the apostle of a republicanism too
broad and pure, no doubt, for this generation of
Frenchmen. But it is the apostle's part to prepare for the future, and to be far in advance of
his age; to foreshadow that which shall rightly
be, long after his own death. Already he sees
the approach to his ideal in the republic
founded. "Kings," he recently said, "are for
nations in their swaddling-clothes; France has
attained her majority." In the "Châtiments"
he declared that in the twentieth century, not
only would America wonderingly exclaim,
"What! I had slaves?" but Europe would also
say, with a shudder, "What! I had kings?"
And so the apostle has become a prophet also;
and these are the titles by which he himself
would be most proud that his fame should de-
scend to posterity.

VII.

JOHN BRIGHT.

A GREATER contrast cannot easily be imagined than that between the subject of the preceding chapter of this series, and that of the present one. Yet, in their very different manners and methods, Victor Hugo and John Bright have labored during their lives for very similar general ends. In his grandiose, florid, rhapsodical way, Victor Hugo has been asserting the individuality and equality of man, the right and necessity of political and social liberty; freedom, too, has been the fervent aspiration, advocated with a strong, straightforward, obstinate, persistent, dogged perseverance, of him who has been graphically called "the great Thor of English politics." The rich and overflowing imagination of the Frenchman has led him to envelop the advocacy of his cause in the ornate forms of allegory, drama, poesy, and satire. The hard English head of Bright has meantime been closely reasoning, framing solid argument, stoutly and

bravely preaching a long unpopular creed from
the hustings and the platform. Victor Hugo's
fancy has been soaring always above and beyond
the region of practical politics, among the air-
castles of an ideal state; John Bright, a product
of British common sense and the commercial
shrewdness of industrial Lancashire, has bounded
his aim to that which he might reasonably hope
to attain at a period not very distant from that
at which he began to agitate. Both have been,
as the current expression is, " ahead of their
time; " but while Hugo has his mental eye fixed
on the twentieth century, at the nearest, John
Bright aims to build greater liberties upon the
broad foundations of the British Constitution as
he goes. Of these two sincere and ardent tribunes of the people, Hugo rages, anathematizes,
loses himself in a bewildering amplitude of magnificent rhetoric; while Bright, though often
strong in invective and stormy indignation,
clearly never loses his self-control, nor allows
himself to overshoot the mark he has set up.

Let us revert to a very critical period in this
country's history; the early summer of 1863.
We were in the midst of the Rebellion; and the
cause of the Union seemed dark indeed. Vicks-

burg, besieged, had not yet fallen. Nor was it scarcely the worst of the misfortunes of the moment, that no decisive step had been taken in the defeat of treason. War with England gravely threatened us. English public opinion was roused angrily, and it seemed overwhelmingly, against us. Palmerston had not long before made a bitterly bellicose speech in the House of Commons. It was, at that moment, an act of rare courage to stand up in the face of English wrath, and defend the Northern cause.

Provided with a letter of introduction to John Bright, from a distinguished member of the United States Senate, I repaired one afternoon in early June, 1863, to the lobby of the House of Commons. Something was to be said, that evening, about American affairs; and this was an especial attraction to an American about to visit the "great debating society" for the first time. In the lobby was a confused crowd of members hurrying in and out, and a still greater crowd of friends, satellites, and anxious constituents. Many faces, become familiar by the photographs of celebrities in the London shop windows, were recognized as the bustle became greater, and the arrivals more numerous, just before the House was called to order. The grave, sallow countenance of Gladstone; Disraeli, with his shock of glossy, jet-black curls, his big nose and thick lips, and springy gait; the jaunty premier, Palmerston, with bushy side-whiskers, twinkling gray eyes, and hat cocked airily on one side of his head; the tall, straight, square form of Sir George Grey; the delicate intellectual face of Sidney Herbert; the round, blond face and flat nose of Lord Stanley (now Earl of Derby); and the pompous, yet rather attractive aspect of Sir John Pakington; these were observed as one and another rapidly passed within the guarded door.

The letter of introduction, with a card, was duly sent in to Mr. Bright, and I took my place in the line of the waiters on the convenience of noble lords and honorable gentlemen. But I had not long to tarry; for presently out came, with a bustling manner and brisk step, a vigorous, full-bodied gentleman, whom I knew at once to be John Bright. He glanced rapidly around upon the line of expectants; and in a moment recognized, no doubt by the American type of the features, the face of which he was in search. Drawing me aside into a window, he began to ask a number of rapid questions about the war, in an abrupt, intent way which was soon seen to be characteristic of him. The state of feeling in the North, Grant's prospects at Vicksburg, the campaign in Virginia, the likelihood of emancipation, were all asked about, the questions following close upon the heels of each preceding response. Then, learning that I desired to see the House in session, he said, " Follow me, and I will get you a better seat than you can secure in the strangers' gallery."

Thereupon he ascended the staircase on the right of the entrance to the House, the attendants bowing low on either side as he passed; and I soon found myself seated in the Speaker's gallery, below that of the strangers, whence there was an excellent view of the House, and where I found myself directly behind a gallery where were seated the Prince of Wales, the Duke of St. Albans, and other notabilities of high rank.

" Shall I hear you this evening, Mr. Bright? " I asked.

" It may be that I shall say something an hour or two hence. I shall, if the American matter comes up. It will be an interesting session, and I advise you to wait."

With which, and with a parting friendly word added, he abruptly left the gallery and I soon after saw him, with his light, quick step, pass up the aisle, and take his seat on the government side, on those benches " below the gangway " reserved for the independent members of the House.

It is related that once a party of Americans entered a studio where a fine portrait, just completed, was standing on the artist's easel.

" Oh," said one of the Americans, " that must be John Bull."

" No," quietly responded the artist, " it's John Bright."

The anecdote forcibly illustrates the truly British physical type of the Quaker orator and statesman. In personal appearance, certainly, he is an Englishman of Englishmen. Robust, though not corpulent, of body; with a round, full face, and bold, straight nose ; his countenance rounded, open, healthfully ruddy, having a remarkable purity of complexion and fine texture of skin; the eyes large, gray, clear, bright, sometimes stern and defiant, but in repose often gentle and kindly ; decision and vigor most plainly expressed in the resolute mouth and firm jaw and chin; a face less mobile than calm and set; the brow broad and white, and arched high at the top; the whole frame strong, well-proportioned, almost massive, indicating great powers of endurance, and giving, even at his present age, no hint of that delicacy of health which has in later years impaired his public activity. In his company, one has a keen sense of his power; one feels himself in the presence of a born leader of men. He holds his head high, and looks you and every one full in the face; and that with a keen, searching glance that rather robs you of your ease. Self-reliance, honesty, pride of intellect, resolution—nay, even intolerance—may be read in his expression.

At the time to which I have referred, John Bright seemed almost absorbed by his interest in the American struggle; and this was, of course, the circumstance which especially attracted Americans to him, and made them eager to hear, see, and read of him. He then stood almost alone as the outspoken advocate of the Union in the House of Commons. Palmerston was openly hostile. Lord John Russell had proved himself unfriendly at the very outset of the war. Gladstone was talking about the South

having become a nation. Roebuck was eagerly
trying to bring about the interference of England, with the co-operation of the French Emperor. Disraeli, who was at heart our friend, at
this period thought it the part of discretion to
be silent. Among the chiefs and orators of the
House, this clear, bold voice of John Bright's
was almost the only one ever heard, defending
the cause of liberty, and uttering, amid all the
gloom, hopeful prophecies. Already, before the
war had been in progress a year, he had, in
words of rare fervor and eloquence, foreshadowed that valiant championship of the North
which he was to display, in stormy times and
serene, from the beginning to the end of the
struggle.

"Whether the Union will be restored or not,"
he said, " or whether the South will achieve an
unhonored independence or not, I know not,
and I predict not. But this I think I know; that
in a few years — a very few years — the twenty
millions of freemen of the North will be thirty
millions, or fifty millions; a population equal
to, or exceeding that of this kingdom. When
that time comes, I pray it may not be said
among them, that, in the darkest hour of their

country's trials, England, the land of their fathers, looked on with icy coldness, and saw unmoved the perils and calamities of her children. As for me, I have but this to say: I am one in this audience, and but one in the citizenship of this country. But if all other tongues are silent, mine shall speak for that policy which gives hope to the bondmen of the South, and tends to generous thoughts and generous words and generous deeds, between the two great nations who speak the English language, and from their origin are alike entitled to the English name!"

John Bright is now (1880) in his sixty-ninth year. He is two years younger than Gladstone and six younger than Lord Beaconsfield; and as English statesmen are a peculiarly vigorous race, and often continue their public activities into the eighties, it may be hoped that he has still some years of labor in the cause of reform before him. His public life began in 1843, when he was thirty-two years of age, in which year he was elected to Parliament by the old historic city of Durham. Four years later, he took his seat for the first time as the representative of the great progressive constituency of Manchester. His career in the House of Commons, therefore, has extended over a period of thirty-seven years.

From the first he was known as a tribune of the people and an apostle of reform. Before entering the House, he had greatly distinguished himself as an orator. He was scarcely twenty when he spoke stirringly to his fellow-townsmen of Rochdale in favor of the great reform bill. He strenuously advocated the abolition of church rates, and was one of the most conspicuous as well as most fervent agitators in favor of putting an end to the unjust corn laws. He preached free trade doctrines, and so soon began to be known as the inveterate foe of landed privilege and aristocratic political control.

When John Bright entered Parliament, it was not merely unpopular, it was fairly odious to be recognized as holding the extreme opinions he boldly avowed. Social ostracism, the distrust and holding aloof of men of all parties, the most contemptuous and hatred-breeding scoffs of almost the entire British press, the horror of the masses of not only educated men, but of the common people, inevitably followed the utterance of radical principles. For years and years, John Bright's name was a bugbear in British politics. He rested under a perpetual cloud of obloquy. The men, who, like noble Richard Cobden, were brave enough to stand by him, shared the stigma cast upon himself. There was, however, in this contumely and avoidance, on the part of party leaders and the party rank and file, something very like fear. It was monstrous that such sentiments should openly be declared in the House of Commons; but was it not also dangerous, especially considering that this commercial Quaker who uttered them could make his voice heard, and was not at all dismayed, and had, moreover, a certain power of character and eloquence?

At all points he was at vigorous variance with the long-settled convictions and prejudices of Old England; and when the Crimean war was imminent, he rose to the greatest height of eloquence he had yet displayed, in opposing the big British armaments, advocating a reduction of the forces, and pleading for a permanent policy of peace and non-intervention in European affairs. So long ago, he foreshadowed the policy which has since been adopted by the wisest heads of the Liberal party. But then it was only his masterly eloquence and strength of character which saved him from the political annihilation which the Liberal chiefs would gladly, in their wrath, have visited upon him. Bright was, perhaps, the only man in Parliament whom the jaunty Palmerston could not laugh or sneer down. Palmerston was then omnipotent in Liberal councils; though if ever there were a Tory at heart, it was he. He used to the uttermost his influence over the dullest prejudices of Englishmen, to disarm this troublesome antagonist, who stood just within his own camp. But the calm reader of the annals of the parliamentary duels of twenty years ago will have no doubt who had the best, at least in intellectual and prophetic points of view, of those formidable frays. Opposition, abuse, vituperation and ridicule, were the food that made this Quaker athlete stronger ; the jeers of Palmerston only endowed him with new vigor and refreshed perseverance.

There came, one day, as if out of a clear sky, a thunderbolt from the Radical corner, which sent dismay through the Liberal ranks. A resolution was sprung upon the House, in favor of household suffrage. The right to vote in England at that time was restricted by a high prop-

erty — that is rental and rating — qualification.
The Radicals sought to reduce this to the mere
occupancy of a house, however small. The battle of household suffrage was then fought with
immense fire and energy by Bright, Cobden,
and that most learned and noble-minded lawyer,
William Page Wood. So splendidly, indeed,
did Page Wood rush to the charge, that when
the vote on the resolution was proceeding, and
Bright met Wood in the lobby, he grasped him
warmly by the hand, and exclaimed, "When
we form a household suffrage cabinet, you shall
be its chancellor."

Eighteen years from that time, it was announced one day that John Bright had become
one of her Majesty's ministers; and quick on
the heels of this intelligence came the news that
William Page Wood had been raised to the cov-
eted woolsack, with the title of Lord Hatherley.
It was not in a household suffrage cabinet; but
despite that, the realization of the prophecy
was a most striking circumstance. Political
prophecy, indeed, seems a real gift with John
Bright. He seems endowed with a remarkable
faculty of prevision. He has foretold many of
the important political changes which have taken

place in recent years in England; and we well
know how his prophecies about the American
Union have turned out. May his more recent
forecast of the great and prosperous destiny before us prove equally true!

In a speech delivered to his constituents John
Bright once declared that he had for a quarter
of a century "endured measureless insult, and
passed through hurricanes of abuse." But after
all, this was only showing one, and that the
darker side of the estimation in which he was
held by the public. If he was the terror and
bête noir of all shades of toryism and prescrip-
tive prejudice, he was also the idol and hope
of that new, vigorous, radical, bold-thinking
class which had rapidly risen to large influence
and electoral power, and which has been called
the "Manchester school." Of the Manchester
school John Bright has ever been the apostle
and the idol. There was one short period, indeed, during which his political disciples trem-
bled lest their great tribune should alienate
himself from them. This was when, on the accession of Gladstone to the Premiership in 1868,
John Bright entered the cabinet as President of
the Board of Trade, and sat as the colleague of

Peelite baronets and whig marquises. It seemed
to the Manchester radical, at that moment, as if
Mirabeau had once more kissed the hand of
Capet, as if Rienzi had again paid court to
Colonna. It was strange to hear of the " Great
Thor " dancing attendance at Windsor, flattered
by the compliments of the Princess Royal, holding obsequious speech with the Queen, and wearing, like a very ill-fitting though finely decked
garment, the title of Right Honorable. The
question arose, has Whiggery gone over to
Bright, or has Bright been absorbed by Whiggery? And indeed, there were signs that the
Quaker statesman wavered at that time in his
radical faith. As a minister, he was cautious,
reticent, and as Delphically official in his utterances as the veriest old-fashioned pupil of statecraft. His opinions seemed to grow lukewarm
and moderate in the official atmosphere, which
was so unlike the invigorating free air of the independent benches he had hitherto breathed.
But, as we look back now at the brief period
during which he held a cabinet portfolio, we
are able to perceive that such a trust had only
affected him, as heavy responsibilities must affect
any man of honest purpose and sensitive patri-

otism. He felt for the first time the gravity of
the task of governing; for the first time saw
questions on all their sides, obstacles in all their
formidableness, and difficulties which he had
probably never before suspected. There was
one other circumstance which will go far to explain John Bright's acceptance of office, and his
caution and moderation when installed in high
place. This was his thorough, and as it proved,
justifiable faith in his chief. He undoubtedly
knew more of Gladstone's real feelings and in-
tentions than any other of their colleagues; and
he felt that Gladstone's aims and his own were
much more nearly identical than people in general suspected. There can be no doubt that
Bright's influence in the cabinet, moreover, which
was large—for his resignation on account of political differences would probably have broken it
— was really devoted to the accomplishment of
reforms which he had long advocated. There
is no question that that article of his creed which
demanded "justice to Ireland," was pressed by
him upon his colleagues, and that he found the
mind of the Premier ripe to receive it. The toil,
the anxieties of office, and perhaps also an un-
dercurrent of consciousness that he was really

out of place, and that his arena was otherwhere, soon wore upon even his massive constitution. His health broke down, and he retired from the Board of Trade; to enter, in 1880, Gladstone's second cabinet as chancellor of the Duchy of Lancaster. No sooner had the restraints of authority been thrown off, and his health to a large degree been restored, than he resumed the great part for which of all living Englishmen he is best fitted — that of a tribune of the people. In his later career, as an independent member of Parliament, there has been no uncertain sound in John Bright's tones. So recently as in the spring of 1879, we find him denouncing in the old, brave, plain-spoken and impressively eloquent way, the existing land tenure of England, and pressing upon English opinion the crying necessity of abolishing, once for all, the laws of primogeniture and entail. Hating war, and a perhaps too intense lover of peace, he has exhausted a most copious vocabulary of vituperation and epithet in denouncing the "spirited foreign policy" of Lord Beaconsfield. Indeed, in John Bright's strong and fiery hatred of traditional abuses and aristocratic privilege, in his fierce scorn of Toryism and all that Toryism

generates, there is fanaticism and intolerance.
His mind is so thoroughly possessed of the ini-
quity of Lord Beaconsfield and all his following,
that he cannot accord them credit for any good
act, for any motives excepting bad and vicious
ones, or even for patriotism, however blundering
and mistaken. Broad and liberal and even cosmopolitan as is the calibre of his mind, here
he becomes a violent partisan and a relentless
enemy; and on this subject he disdains to measure his words. It requires a large amount of
courage for a man to stand up in such a country
as England — a proud land, believing intensely
in itself, rather contemptuous of foreign methods,
customs, and laws; a land which is, perhaps,
best of all described as " insular " — and praise
another country at the expense of his own; especially, to praise another country which his
own has always been in the habit of looking
down upon and condescending towards, and
patronizing by fits and starts. Yet this John
Bright has done more than once; and more emphatically than ever, within the past few months.
In the most glowing tribute which was perhaps
ever paid to the United States by a foreigner,
he contrasted our prosperity with England's

depression, our democratic government with England's expensive paraphernalia of royalty, our little army with England's costly legions, the freedom of our soil with England's law-fettered land monopoly, our freedom from alliances, diplomatic complications, and burdensome colonies, with England's constant embroilment in European politics, and England's perpetual necessity to defend distant possessions at an enormous cost of blood and money, and ever widening care and responsibility. Nor did John Bright point this contrast with all the rich wealth of his Saxon eloquence without a purpose. He does not hesitate to hold America up to England as an example, in many of its features to be followed. He would have English land liberated; he would withdraw her from the entangling alliances of the continent; he would reduce her armaments; he would have her cease to acquire new territory in savage and semi-civilized lands; it is not certain that he would not see with satisfaction her severance from the burdens of Indian empire; he would extend the suffrage, and still further reform the House of Commons, so that it might be more truly than now the representative body of the great masses of the people.

There has always been much difference of opinion as to which is the greater orator, Gladstone, Beaconsfield, or John Bright. The contrast between the eloquence of the three is very marked; by contrast only can their various oratorical powers be compared. But, as time has gone on, the numbers of those who give the preeminence in this respect to John Bright have rapidly increased. There is a charm of musical sweetness, and a glow of warmth, of earnestness and enthusiasm, about Gladstone's speeches, which certainly make one hesitate to judge any one his superior in eloquence. There is a finish, a subtlety and grace, a sparkle and a fine-edged wit about Beaconsfield's addresses, which make him a master among parliamentary speakers, and leave him *facile princeps* in his own peculiar style of forensic oratory. Bright's eloquence, however, is a marvellous exhibition of simplicity combined with strength, of absolute perfection of language, of measured ease and deliberation, of natural gifts of a very high order most carefully trained and finished, of powerful appeal to the average common sense, and of the most skilful fitting of the utterance to the thought. The first impression of Bright, as amid the most absolute stillness he rises, with every eye upon him and every ear eagerly intent, to address the House of Commons, is far more striking than the first impression made by either of his oratorical rivals. His presence at once attracts and more than satisfies the eye. His snow-white, flowing hair, his rotund form, his erect posture, his perfect self-possession, his large, bright gray eye, his clear, strong voice that immediately charms the ear, take possession of one at the very outset of his address. As, with measured sentences, he proceeds, you are constantly struck by the simplicity, directness, purity, and fitness of every word and every sentence. " His language," says a shrewd observer, " is more thoroughly and racily English than that of any speaker in either House." Unlike many English orators, Bright rarely quotes from the classics. Robert Lowe loads down his harangues with a wearying wealth of quotations from Virgil and Horace, Homer and Herodotus. Gladstone cannot resist the temptation to often adorn his addresses with the images of his beloved Greek masters. Beaconsfield not seldom turns a smooth joke with an apt borrowing from the Latin. At least equal to either of these in the abundance, the beauty, and the fitness of his illustrations, Bright almost invariably draws them from two main sources. He either finds in the master-pieces of English poetry — Shakespeare, Chaucer, Milton, Spenser — the materials for his similes; or he resorts for this purpose to the Bible. No one can have read the best specimens of English and American eloquence, without having observed what telling use can be made, before either a select or a miscellaneous assemblage, of Biblical allusions. Illustrations from that high and universally familiar source have a power peculiarly their own; and certainly no orator has ever made more powerful use of them than John Bright. Could there ever have been anything, for instance, more effective than when, during the debate on the Reform Bill of 1866, he made use of the story of David's escape from Achish, King of Gath, to brand the Liberal bolters as inhabitants of the "Cave of Adullam." From that time forth, the "Adullamites" were as much a recognized party name as Whig or Tory. More recently, speaking of the grumbling discontent of the Tories at Gladstone's policy, he humorously declared that, "had they been in the wilderness, they would

have complained of the ten commandments."
The fitness and force of his illustrations are
equally apparent whether Bright draws them from
secular legend, or literature, or from common,
every-day things and sayings. Like Disraeli, he
is a notable inventor of nicknames and epithets;
and hesitates as little to apply them right and
left. He once alluded very effectively to Disraeli as " the mystery man of the ministry; " on
another occasion, about the period of the " Adul-
lamite " defection from the Liberals, he referred
to Mr. Lowe and Mr. Horsman combined as a
" Scotch terrier, of which no one could with cer-
tainty say which was the head and which the
tail." Not less stinging was his satire upon the
Tory minister, Sir Charles Adderly, that " I hope
he thought he was telling the truth; but he is
rather a dull man, and is liable to make blun-
ders." Bright is always readily severe upon
pride of ancestry; and once said of the ancestors
of a man who boasted that they had come over
with the Conqueror, that " I never heard that
they did anything else." Soon after John Bright
had yielded to the illness which compelled his
retiring from the cabinet, a Tory lordling took
occasion to remark in public that Providence, in

order to punish Bright for the misuse of his talents, had afflicted him with a disease of the brain. " It may be so," said Bright in the House of Commons, after his recovery; "but in any case, it will be some consolation to the friends and family of the noble lord to know, that the disease is one which even Providence could not inflict upon him ! " Sometimes Bright's images rise into regions of grandeur ; and at such times, they never pass into that of bathos, though sometimes approaching near it. When the negotiations were going on at Vienna, with a view of closing the Crimean War, Bright made a powerful speech in favor of peace, in the course of which he used the finest image, perhaps, that he ever uttered. " The Angel of Death," he said, with deep, slow, solemn voice and uplifted hand, " has been abroad throughout the land ; you may almost hear the beating of his wings ! " " That was a noble idea ! " exclaimed Cobden, meeting him afterwards in the lobby. " But if you had said the ' flapping ' of his wings, the House would have roared you down with laughter." Many other passages of the most genuine eloquence are quoted from Bright's speeches; especially two, in one of which he pathetically

pictured the wrongs of Ireland, and in the other
he a few years ago defended his course in Parliament before his constituents at Birmingham.
He has always seemed to take special delight in
throwing ridicule on Disraeli; and having spoken of him as the "mystery man," he afterwards
somewhat more roughly characterized him as
"the mountebank with a pill for the earth-
quake." A very marked trait of Bright's eloquence is its simple, but profound and often
thrilling pathos. His speeches, indeed, have
sometimes been described as monotonously
sombre and gloomy; an effect only relieved by
the vivacity of his manner and gesture. But in
recent years this sombreness has become less
and less noticeable, as he has emerged from the
obloquy and hatred inspired by his early and
loud-voiced radicalism, and has become a real
political power in the land. Meanwhile his
power in the use of pathos has ripened and
deepened. "For the expression of pathos,"
says an English writer, "there are inexpressibly
touching tones in his voice; tones which carry
right to the listener's heart the tender thoughts
that come glowing from the speaker's, and are
clad in simple words as they pass his tongue."

Especially is this so, when, as is often the case, he is pleading the cause of the oppressed, or "denouncing a threatened wrong." The boldness and aggressiveness of his oratory have been already illustrated by his epithets and his personal characterizations. "Mr. Bright's rhetoric," says one, "has certainly a great deal of the clenched fist in it; and when it exhibits the open hand, it is usually to administer a slap in the face." But if a man's eloquence may be tested by its palpable results, by its hold upon the assemblies it addresses, by its conversions and inspiration of multitudes, by its quotable properties, by its use of every sub-art of oratory, from appropriateness of gesture and fitness of language to the skilful wielding of rhetoric, sarcasm, humor, pathos, scorn, persuasiveness, and logical force, it is very certain that John Bright is one of the world's great orators.

Is John Bright also a statesman? He once himself said that the name of statesman was so often misapplied, and has taken on so often an unenviable significance, that he cared very little to have it applied to him. A statesman of the old-fashioned, official, mysterious, office-drilled, adroitly managing, compromising sort, he cer-

tainly is not. No man could be more unlike
Palmerston, or Russell, or Pitt, or even Sir Robert Peel, than he. His experience of official
responsibility was, as has been seen, brief, and
not very fruitful in practical evidences of administrative capacity. Indeed, the Board of Trade
scarcely furnishes a scope for broad measures
of public policy, or widely extending reforms.
John Bright's main use in the Cabinet, indeed,
was as a participant in its general councils; as
the adviser of Gladstone in such imperial matters
as the disestablishment of the Irish church, and
the abolition of purchase in the British army.
He has not been himself the originator of many
important measures, nor the author of many
momentous bills. But in another sense, John
Bright may claim the title of statesman in its
best and highest meaning. He is surely not,
like Victor Hugo, a declaimer, prophet, apostle
only. His view of politics and events is much
more Englishly practical. Radical and sometimes extreme as his public life has been, it has
had a strong leaven of good sense, and has often
shown a keen discrimination of what has been
and what has not been possible to attain. He
has seldom or never lost himself in fine dreams

of an ideal future; while yet he has not, like the technical statesman, confined himself to the calculation and detail of the present. His sweep of vision has been broad, and before him, more than behind or around him. His mind has been clear outside of and above considerations of the precedents and usages of the past. He has ever abhorred the Tory idea that whatever is, is right. He has boldly aimed to destroy, but he has always known very well what he would put in place of the thing destroyed. His bump of political veneration is small indeed; but he is not by any means a revolutionist pure and simple. There can be no doubt, indeed, that John Bright has set an indelible mark on the legislation of his time; that his influence has been large in effecting not only broad, but perfectly practicable reforms. He had much to do with bringing about the repeal of the corn laws. He proposed an amendment to the measure for abolishing church rates, which went far towards making it an effective instrument. A profound student of India, and the relations of that great dependency to the British Empire, he has more than once brought about modifications in its government which have vastly improved it.

He was one of the moving spirits who succeeded in securing the famous Cobden treaty of commerce with France; and from his lips came the earliest proposal of an arbitration court for settling the Alabama difficulty between England and the United States. Nor can it be justly denied that his speeches on the Eastern question, though he sat with a hopeless minority on the opposition benches, have had a powerful effect in shaping, by the formation and inspiration of public opinion, England's foreign policy.

There was, therefore, much injustice in the epigram of one of his opponents, that John Bright "possesses Cicero's eloquence, and Catiline's love of conspiracy." No man could be further from assuming the rôle of a conspirator. Whatever Bright has said or done has been open and above board. While sometimes bitter in his denunciation of royal extravagance, he has never been disloyal to the person of the Queen; whose virtues, on the other hand, he has often extolled with warm and evidently sincere panegyric. While he has boldly spoken of the House of Lords in contemptuous tones, as the last refuge of political ignorance and passion, it is doubtful whether he would engage in a crusade against the existence of that body; lest the evils brought about by that overturning should prove to overweigh the good.

His eloquence has always captivated, and often convinced the multitudes who have thronged everywhere to hear him; his arduous and enthusiastic service in the cause of the oppressed has endeared him to thousands who never heard his clear, clarion voice, or beheld his flowing white hair and his sturdy English frame; while his friendship, so thoroughly tried, for his kinsmen across the seas, will yield him as great honor from future generations of Americans as the name of Chatham receives from ours.

VIII.

THREE EMPERORS.

OF the many World's Exhibitions that have taken place within the past thirty years, perhaps the one which most deeply impressed those who witnessed it, and which will linger longest in the memory of men, was that held at Paris in the summer of 1867. It was not, perhaps, that its display of the products of human industries and arts was the most various and elaborate; or that the magnificence of the buildings and grounds which included these exceeded that of other exhibitions; or because of the recreations which Paris so bountifully — and at such extraordinary prices — provided its myriad guests of all nations. The distinctive feature of the exhibition of 1867 — that which made it altogether exceptional, unique, unprecedented — was its display of human and personal pageantry. Napoleon III., then apparently at the height of his power and imperial splendor, employed one masterly device to lend unrivalled

glory to the festival. To it he lured in turn
nearly every considerable potentate of the earth.
Emperors, Sultans, Shahs, were his daily guests.
Paris revelled in a perpetual round of gorgeous
fêtes, of which the central figures were the
greatest rulers of Europe and Asia. The stranger abiding there saw pass before him, as in a
panorama, the personified might of the nations,
surrounded by all the traditional paraphernalia
of majesty, until he who was but a King of Portugal, or a Grand Duke of Mecklenburg, passed
almost unnoticed amid the loftier figures.

And among these potentates, who thus lent
themselves to reflect a greater lustre upon the
crown of the *parvenu* Bonaparte (whom once
they had disdainfully refused to recognize at all),
by all odds the most conspicuous were the three
monarchs who still, at seventeen years' distance, rule the three most powerful empires of
continental Europe. The Czar Alexander and
King William of Prussia (now Emperor of Germany) were in Paris at the same time, attended
by their two famous chancellors, Gortschakoff
and Bismarck, and accompanied by their stalwart sons and heirs; and it was my fortune to
see them both, more than once, riding through

the streets beside the Emperor Napoleon, in one
of those enormous old-fashioned royal coaches
which had been dragged out of their dusty obscurity to lend an air of ancient royalty to the
occasion. The Emperor Francis Joseph of Austria came later, alone; and received, unsharing it
with others, the profuse hospitalities of his "well-
beloved brother" of France. However strongly
imbued he might be with Republican ideas, no
American could witness these hereditary rulers of
men without curiosity and interest. There is a romance about kingship, to the citizen of a distant
republic, which the subjects of kings never feel.
It does not partake of awe, and has no essence
of loyalty to the principle of heredity in power.
It is purely picturesque; to see a famous sovereign is like finding the hero of an old romance
in real life. The contrast, too, between the
stately accessories that surround a king, the
ceremonial dignities, the military accompani-
ments, and the simplicity of republican custom,
adds its glamour to the curiosity thus aroused
and gratified. It was, therefore, with eagerness
that I availed myself of the opportunity not only
to witness the pageantry with which these sovereigns appeared, but to scrutinize their features,

to observe their movements, to watch the changing expressions of their countenances. The memory of their long descent from rude rulers and doughty warriors and of their famous predecessors — of Rurick and Rudolph, of Frederick Von Zollern and Vater Fritz, of Peter the Great and the wicked Catherine, of Maria Theresa and Frederick Barbarossa — aided much to intensify the gratification I felt at beholding these men made great by right of birth.

Much more interesting do these three potentates become, when it is added that each is a man of decided ability and of conspicuous virtues. We will not stop to discuss the problem of the heredity of brains, or the transmission of mental qualities in the blood; or to decide whether or not the royal lines of Europe prove or disprove Mr. Galton's attractive and ingenious theory. It is at least certain that, in our own day, the realms of Europe are remarkably fortunate in the abilities and personal characters of their royal heads. No nation is to-day cursed by a very bad or a very imbecile ruler. Since the deposition of Bomba in Naples and of Isabella in Spain, no crying scandal has clung to a European throne. On the other hand, a large majority of the sovereigns betray more than average capacity, and more than ordinarily good personal traits. The Queen of England is a model of strong good sense and domestic virtue. The Kings of Italy, Portugal, Spain, and Belgium are wise and liberal rulers, content to be constitutional, and to govern according to the wishes of their people. The King of Sweden is a man of culture, and politically sagacious as well as a talented poet. The King of Denmark is a mild and popular monarch, a pattern Scandinavian father of a well-brought-up family of charming children. The King of Holland is rather dull, but not aggressively offensive to his subjects. The King of Bavaria is a musical monomaniac, but has very little governing to do, being relieved mostly of such cares by his subordination to the German Empire. The last may also be said of the Kings of Würtemberg and Saxony, who are, moreover, estimable and amiable German gentlemen, sympathetic with the artistic tastes of their subjects, and inspiring a patriarchal respect and affection in their hearts.

Returning to the trio of Emperors, there can be no doubt of their excellence of personal traits,

their more than common ability, or the affection
with which they are regarded by the millions
whom they rule. In these modern and revolutionary days, the individual characters of hereditary monarchs count, perhaps, for less and less
every year. But no one will question that the
characters of the three Emperors have had very
much to do with current events in Europe during the past quarter of a century. Two of them
are still absolute despots; the third was so during the first eighteen years of his reign. It is
certain that it was the Czar's personal act to
emancipate the serfs; that it was largely owing
to William's military tastes and training that
Prussia became the head of a unified Germany;
and that a less wise or less patriotic sovereign
than Francis Joseph might have failed to conciliate Hungary, and have refused to grant a constitution to his dual realm.

Of the Imperial trio, William of Germany is
at once the senior in point of age, and the junior
in the number of years that he has reigned;
while Francis Joseph is at once the youngest
man and the oldest sovereign. Francis Joseph
is about fifty, ascended the throne in 1848, and
has reigned nearly thirty-two years. William is

eighty-three, ascended the throne in 1862, and has reigned eighteen years. Alexander is sixty-two, ascended the throne in 1855, and has reigned just a quarter of a century.

While the sovereigns of Russia and Austria are, in personal appearance and bearing, modern Emperors, William of Germany has a certain quaint air and flavor about him of real old-time, typical royalty. His big, stalwart, strongly knit frame, which at eighty-four sustains bravely the fatigue of military pageantry and the crowding business of a vast state; his lofty, knightly, yet courteous bearing; his clear, cold, slowly gazing light-blue eye; his finely arched and tufted eyebrows of snowy white; his sweeping military mustache; his strong, broad chin and jaw, and thin lips; his air of having ever the consciousness of majesty; his voice, with its commanding tones, its thick Berlinese accent, its slow and measured cadence, that of one who chooses his words and expects to be listened to; his faultless memory, a trait that the warrior sovereigns of old cultivated and prided themselves upon; his fondness for the table, for the lusty sports of the Fatherland, for domestic reunions, for military show and the grim realities of war, — all

stamp him as the stalwart monarch of a stalwart
people, the successor of Hochmeisters and Kur-
fürsts, who boldly typifies alike the physical and
the mental traits of his rough and stormy ancestors. With the proud bearing of a knight of
the Hospitallers, his head ever high in air, William has the thorough patriarchal good-nature
of the Teuton. Anecdotes are related of him,
exceedingly expressive of his quaint, blunt,
homely character, which we should never think
of hearing related of his brother Emperors.
Once at a state ball, he saw a young officer
rather rudely turn his back on an English lady
of rank. The Emperor strode up to him, took
him by the shoulder, and turned him sharply
round. "Never turn your back to a lady, sir,"
he said in his thick, loud voice. On another
occasion, he observed an officer dancing awk-
wardly; and at once sent an aide to him, with
the command that he must not dance again till
he could dance better. The kindliness of his
nature — a rough, bearish, but very genuine
kindliness — is illustrated by a hundred anecdotes always afloat in Germany. Once, not long
after the splendid victory of Sadowa, he was
strolling through the gardens of the Kursaal at

Ems, when he met an old soldier, who had been badly wounded on the Bohemian battle-field, hobbling along with difficulty on his crutches. The old soldier, on perceiving his sovereign, hastily took off his hat, which fell from his hands to the ground. William at once stooped, picked up the hat, and put it upon the veteran's head. The soldier began to deprecate a favor of which he thought himself unworthy. "Tut, tut, my worthy man," replied the King, "William reigns at Berlin; but this day he is happy to serve at Ems."

The German Emperor's habits are such as may be inferred from the slight glimpse of his traits already given. At eighty-three he is to all appearance as hale and vigorous, as clear of intellect and as cheerful in disposition, as capable of enduring physical fatigue, as indefatigable in the performance of his political and military tasks, as he was when he came to the throne. His appetite is still Teutonic in its capacity, and he still, as for years, goes sturdily through the severe routine of every day, which brims with employment for him. He may be seen periodically inspecting his pet regiments, sometimes seated on his big white horse, remaining firmly

fixed in the saddle for hours together, and sometimes on foot, striding with strong tread athwart
the front of a long line of grenadiers, in the
Schloss-Platz at Potsdam. William is and always
has been an early riser. Leaving a by no means
luxurious couch with the dawn, his first act is to
read a chapter in the Bible. This betrays to us
one of his most conspicuous traits. Like his
great chancellor, Bismarck, the Emperor is a
firm believer in Protestant Christianity. His
piety, too, has all the simplicity and directness
of a nature too frank and honest ever to assume
religious faith as a cloak. Those who remember
his remarkable despatches to his wife from the
seat of war in 1870, cannot have failed to be
struck with the constant allusions to his gratitude to God, and the reference of events to the
divine source. There was something quite Crom-
wellian in their blunt utterance of fervidly pious
faith; nor did any one question that all that he
expressed, he deeply felt.

Having performed his devotions the Emperor,
booted, spurred, and in the military costume he
almost invariably wears, goes into his study, a
room looking out upon the square in front of the
palace. From its window he may, if he chooses,

derive daily inspiration from the noble eques-
trian statue of the great Frederic, that stands in
the square. He takes his place at a little desk
in the corner of the study, where a small cup of
coffee is served to him, after partaking of which
he rapidly scans the morning newspapers. The
heavy mail which has just arrived next claims
his attention, and it is no slight task to go
through it. He makes notes of instructions to
his secretaries on the envelopes, and places them
in the large bags which are ready to his hand on
the floor. The first audience is given to an aide-
de-camp, who makes each morning a report on
the state of the garrisons in Berlin; and then the
Emperor gives the aide a list of the persons he
will receive. It is now perhaps half-past nine,
and time for breakfast. William proceeds to the
Empress's apartments, and greets her for the first
time in the day; and there the Imperial couple
sit down to a substantial German breakfast.
While at table, the bill of fare for dinner is
brought, inspected, and approved. The venerable pair almost invariably breakfast alone. The
repast leisurely discussed and over, they go
down into the luxurious saloons that overlook
the Platz. Here they are joined by the Crown

Prince and Princess, and the Empress reads aloud an hour or two, while her lord sits in a luxurious arm-chair. Later in the morning, the Emperor goes to his official reception-room, and there receives the officers of his household, persons to whom he has accorded an audience, ministers, ambassadors, and military officers. Then follows, in the Emperor's presence, the Cabinet council. He sits at the head of a long table, covered with green baize, surrounded by his advisers; and there the destinies of Germany and Europe are discussed, and mighty events have now and then been decreed. This room, also, looks out upon the spacious Platz; and often, in the middle of the day, may the venerable monarch be seen standing at one of the windows, looking out at the people passing to and fro, and chivalrously returning their respectful obeisances. If a military company marches by, he straightens up, buttons his military coat to the throat, and with erect, martial bearing, gives it the regulation salute. The back of the day's work is broken by three o'clock, by which time the Emperor has lightly lunched on black bread, a bit of cold meat, and a glass or two of Moselle. He then begins to take his ease, and indulge in the lighter duties and pleasures of royalty. He spends, perhaps, an hour or two looking at his books and maps, examining his new works of art, of which he is passionately fond, and chatting with his wife or son. Then, seated in an open carriage, drawn by a span of coal-black horses, he takes a rapid drive through the Under den Linden, and around the Thiergarten. Everywhere he is received with unmistakable signs of the veneration and affection of his subjects; to their greetings he responds with smiles and gracious wavings of his hand. No sooner has he returned to the palace than he finds himself closeted with Bismarck, who has brought the daily report of the state of the German Empire. It is no doubt a relief when the grim chancellor retires, and his somewhat tired majesty may sit down to a frugal but plenteous dinner, of which he partakes alone with the Empress. It is only occasionally that there are guests at the table; at these rare times the guests are few. It is a thoroughly quiet, simple, domestic meal. The brief interval between dinner and the opera or theatre is spent in reading letters and telegrams, and conferring with secretaries, — the lingering remains of the state toils of the day. William is intensely fond both of the opera and the drama. Nearly all his evenings are spent at one or the other; and there alone, it would appear, can he entirely throw aside the burdens and cares of sovereignty, and thoroughly enjoy himself. He is quite German in his enthusiasm for music, and it is a serious obstacle which can keep him away from the first representation of a masterpiece by a famous composer.

The Emperor William prides himself on being "the father of his people." He bears himself easily and naturally in the rôle of a royal patriarch. His paternal care and solicitude for his subjects are displayed alike in the assiduity with which he devotes his labors to matters of state, and in the grave gentleness with which he responds to their salutations. There are indulgence and kindness in his patriarchal bearing; but the Prussians have long since learned that, though genial, his rule is thoroughly autocratic. There is at least, in the palace, no idea of the concession of popular liberties. When his subjects appear to be getting impatient of the restraints of autocratic government, and demand some modicum of constitutional freedom, the venerable monarch seems to smile a lofty smile, and has the air of saying, "Why, really, my children, you are crying for the moon!" Among all the good things William has done for Prussia and for Germany, among all the glories and powers that he has won for them, it would be difficult to find a single act designed to share with the people the government of the nation. He is a despot, though a genial and loving despot; and Germany must probably await the advent of a less popular ruler, before she can hope to win that freedom which seems to us the only proper complement and crowning of her unity.

Between the stalwart, bluff, and hearty old German Emperor, and his nephew, the Czar of the Russias, the contrast is very striking. It is true that Alexander II. had a German mother (William's sister), received his education in Germany, and in tastes and character seems more of the mild and studious German type than of that of the rude, bold Russian. In many of the kingly qualities of William, however, he is quite wanting; while he has neither the haughty and cruel spirit of his father, the Czar Nicholas, nor the active temperament and gracious bearing of his uncle, the Czar Alexander I. He is perhaps the gentlest and most humane and best meaning sovereign who ever sat on the Muscovite throne. His inclinations have always been manifestly for peace, progress, and improvement. So little did he inherit of the military taste and spirit of his ancestry, that Nicholas his father disliked, almost despised him, and had at one time serious thoughts of excluding him from the succession. There can be little doubt that Alexander has always shrunk from making war, and that he has never without reluctance entered upon it. His dislike of parade and show, of figuring at reviews and attending military pageants, is well known. He always avoids them when it is possible. His almost feminine timidity and nervousness have long been remarked. There have been many incidents of his life which indicate that personal courage is not one of his conspicuous traits. The various attempts which have been made upon his life have shattered his composure, and rendered him a constant prey to the dread of sudden and violent death. Sometimes this dread has so haunted him as to well-nigh deprive him of reason. He is a confirmed hypochondriac. It is very rarely that a smile flits across his handsome, but most melancholy countenance. This sadness of feature is greatly increased of late; at sixty-three, he looks seventy. His once rich brown hair, and military mustache and whiskers, are thin, shaggy, and gray; deep lines, as of care and sorrow, cross his face; his air is that of a man long hunted, and desperately weary of being hunted. Uneasy, indeed, lies at least this head that wears the proud crown of Rurick. Perhaps there is no more unhappy man in all Russia than its ruler. There is more than one cause for the miserable existence which, in sombre contrast with the hearty enjoyment of life and of majesty experienced by the German Emperor, is led by the mighty potentate of Russia. Time was when the motto of every Russian was, " My life for the Czar! " His person was sacred, as his will was law. But the times have changed. The vast, occult conspiracy of Nihilism has literally turned thousands of Russian hands against the heart of him who is their Pope as well as their sovereign. His despotism is in these days more than ever " tempered by assassination." The Czar lives daily in just terror of secret conspiracy. Death may lurk in his food, beneath the floor of his palace, in the very letters he opens, behind the curtains of his bed. The effect of this perpetual threat, at all hours and in all places, upon a finely strung, nervous, timid, sensitive organization as is that of the Czar, may be imagined. But, aside from this Damocles' sword, forever suspended above his head, the Czar is tortured by the unruly conduct of his son and heir, a young man in whom is revived the old, rough, fierce, overbearing, warlike spirit of the haughty house of Romanoff. He is perplexed by the clamors of his nobles; he is driven into courses from which he is averse, by the powerful " Old Russia " party; the cares of government press heavily upon him; the chief joy of his life, his only daughter, lives in a distant and unfriendly country; his feeble health is an almost constant torment.

The resources and tastes of the Czar happily in some degree mitigate the darker aspects and influences of his life. He is polished and scholarly, fond of books, enjoys best of all the hours when he is left in solitude and quiet, in the midst of his family, in his library, and amid the luxurious retreats which it is one of the few privileges of his rank to possess. When out of sight of the world, and among trusted friends, he loses something of his melancholy, and enters into the pastime of the hour with gentle zest. His manners, while grave and quiet, are not dignified. He quite lacks the hauteur of his father Nicholas. There is, however, a certain kindliness in his bearing which wins the hearts of those who are permitted to approach near enough to discover his real self. " He produces the impression," says an English writer who has often seen him, " that one would like to know him better, if only he were not an Emperor. There is something extremely sympathetic about him." Alexander is not devoid entirely of a taste for the robust sports of his hardy northern land. He is fond of a good horse; and until within a few years was somewhat noted as a huntsman, having achieved much success in the hunting of bears. But in these days, to go hunting would be to add to the chances of assassination. Not many years ago, one of the Czar's favorite pastimes was to walk, almost or quite unattended, through the streets of his capital, or in the gardens surrounding his palace. This, too, he has given up, since the repeated attempts upon his life. More and more each year he inclines to the seclusion of a recluse. His sleep is uneasy and troubled. At table he is abstemious and

simple; it is only on the occasion of a state dinner that the Imperial table groans with the good
things brought to the ice-bound capital from
southern and western Europe. He seldom stays
long in the brilliant court balls which ever and
anon break the usual solemn silence of the Winter Palace; and his visits to the opera become
more rare every year. When he goes out now,
it is in his carriage or drosky, swiftly driven,
and flanked on either side by heavily armed and
fierce-looking mounted Cossacks. If he travels
by rail, it is in a closely shut compartment, and
only after every precaution has been taken to
keep the track clear and the way safe.

During his long and eventful reign, the Czar
Alexander has many times shown his desire,
even his anxiety, to confer solid benefits upon
his people. This inclination, indeed, appeared
almost immediately after he ascended the throne.
Unlike Nicholas, his disposition was liberal and
magnanimous; it was perhaps the observation
of his father's unbending cruelty and remorse-
less rule, that actuated him to diverge so soon
and so completely from his father's policy. He
established many reforms in the public administration during the early years of his reign; and

thus soon won that hostility of the nobles, and
of the warlike and arbitrary " old Russia " party,
which has been kept alive ever since. He
brought about improvements in the system of
education in Russia, and freed the universities
from some of the odious restrictions imposed on
them by Nicholas; he relieved the military pres-
sure which had existed over civil affairs; and he
abolished the most irksome laws restricting the
Russian press. Towards the inveterately discon-
tented Poles he manifested a studied gentleness
and leniency; granting a universal amnesty in
the second year of his reign, and removing many
of the despotic measures that weighed upon the
unhappy subject kingdom.   Then came the
noblest of all his acts, — an act which must preserve for him a loftier and sweeter renown than
attaches to the name of any other Russian
autocrat. Suddenly, without consultation with
family or nobles, he struck the shackles from the
swarming millions of serfs who toiled beneath
the yoke of the proud, cruel, and indolent Russian landed proprietors. To be sure, this emancipation was far from complete; nay, is not by
any means complete to this day. But it was
nevertheless a bold and grand act, the outcome

of a lofty impulse; and it may be fairly said that as far as it lay in the Czar Alexander's power to do it, the whole body of Russian serfdom was made free.

The later features of his reign, unfortunately, have not sustained its wise and brave beginnings. The attempts upon his life, the rise and formidable growth of Nihilism, the influence of strong wills like that of Gortschakoff and of grand dukes and despotic nobles, acting upon a nervous and unhappy temperament, have resulted in inducing Alexander too often to resort to the old, hard, cruel methods of his predecessors. The press has again become the slave of rigid censorship; Siberia once more receives her miserable quota of victims year by year; the Poles feel, as of old, the terrors of the quiet that reigns, under Russian bayonets, at Warsaw; and the great cities scarcely breathe, under the oppression of the stern martial law which has been proclaimed over them. The Czar seems, indeed, in these latter days, quite powerless, autocrat as he is, to do those things for his people which his own liberal and generous impulses would naturally prompt; and we can scarcely conceive of a more wretched situation than that of a well-disposed arbitrary monarch, who finds himself responsible for all the oppressions and injustices that are done to his people, and yet who is unable to lift his hand to protect them from it.

The Emperor Francis Joseph of Austria is a good and wise sovereign, and an amiable and high-minded gentleman. No living European ruler more thoroughly deserves the affections of his subjects and the respect of the world. Although only fifty years of age, he has reigned thirty-two years; and those years have been full of vicissitude, turmoil, misfortune, and struggle with him. His task has been more difficult than that of any other European potentate; and he has acquitted it with a degree of judgment, tact, sincere patriotism, and patience, which stamp him as one of the most able hereditary governors of men now living. Called to rule over a polyglot empire, composed of five or six different and mutually jealous races, each pulling against the others, each clamoring for that which it was contrary to the interests of the others to concede, his course has been through the most dangerous passes and channels, amid constantly confronting perils. If he yielded to the demands of the Czechs, he offended the Germans;

if German influence was uppermost in his councils, Hungary was rebellious. Besides these internal perplexities, he had the hereditary external complications and quarrels of the Empire on
his hands. It was his task to maintain the position of Austria as a great power; to make exi-
gent alliances, at times to enter into wars from
which he emerged discomfited, beaten, and de-
prived of territories. Amid all these troubles,
the Emperor Francis Joseph has borne himself
with dignity, prudence, self-control, and, more
than once, with a fine spirit of self-sacrifice,
when his prerogatives as a monarch were to be
restricted and lessened for the benefit of his
subjects.

Francis Joseph is perhaps the only potentate
who has passed from the position of a despot
into that of a constitutional sovereign, without
being forced to do so by actual revolution. It
is to his eternal honor that he has cheerfully
and loyally given constitutional freedom to all
his subjects; that under his beneficent sway,
Austria to-day enjoys a degree of political and
social liberty which places her far in the van of
her sister empires of Russia and Germany. The
wisdom of his self-abnegating policy is seen in

the comparative content in which the diverse
populations of Austro-Hungary now dwell together. Hungary, once stormily insurgent, is
the most loyal of his Imperial dominions, the
strongest support to his throne. Francis Joseph
has pursued this enlightened course with great
firmness and steadfastness, against formidable
obstacles. His family, the court, his noble
counsellors, have often urgently opposed the
conciliatory steps which he has nevertheless
boldly taken. With conspicuous magnanimity,
he accepted as his chancellor the Hungarian
Count Andrassy, upon whose head the Emperor
himself had once been obliged to set a price, as
a traitor and rebel. When he went to Pesth to
be crowned King of Hungary with the ancient
iron diadem, he visited the stubborn old patriot,
Francis Deak, in his garret, and urged him — in
vain — to accept the marked favors which it is
the privilege of royalty to bestow. His treatment of Italy, who took from him some of his
fairest provinces, has been exceedingly generous and friendly; his relations with other potentates have always seemed to be seized by
Francis Joseph as opportunities to maintain the
peace of Europe. Never once, since Austria

became a constitutional state, has he evinced any restiveness under the new condition, or any desire to return to arbitrary methods. Yet in his veins courses the blood of the haughty Hapsburgs, — the proudest, cruelest, most despotic race of monarchs, on the whole, who have ever held sway in Europe, unless we except the half-barbarous descendants of Othman and the second Mahomet. Nor is Francis Joseph less proud than his Imperial successors. It must have deeply wounded him to lose, first Milan and Lombardy, and then, seven years later, his still fairer appanage of Venice; to see the conquering legions of Prussia encamping on his Bohemian fields; to concede constitutional liberty to that truculent and restless Hungary which came near despoiling him of his crown almost as soon as it had been placed upon his head. Unlike the Bourbons, however, he has proved himself able and willing to learn the lessons taught by repeated misfortune. In a better and higher sense, therefore, than the term can be applied to the Emperor William, Francis Joseph has been " the father of his people; " sacrificing his pride and his power for their sake.

In person, Francis Joseph is of medium height,

slim, erect, and with a graceful bearing. His reddish brown hair is scant on the crown, the bareness of which gives an appearance of unusual size to the high, round forehead. The hair is always cropped as close to the round head as is the fashion with our college youth in summer time. The face is a long, well-filled-out oval; each cheek is covered with very heavy and long reddish brown whiskers, which fall almost to the breast. The Emperor has the true protruding " Hapsburg lip," which has been a marked peculiarity of the Austrian sovereigns for many generations; but it is almost concealed by a long sweeping military mustache, the ends of which are brushed jauntily upward. The chin is round and handsome; the nose straight and strong; the large dark gray eyes are grave and serious, but not unkindly in expression. So, too, his bearing is always full of sedateness and quiet dignity, by no means obtrusively haughty, his imperial rank sitting easily and naturally upon him. Unlike the Czar, he is by no means fond of solitude, but like the Czar, he has little taste for state pageantry or court festivities. He used to be fond of the theatre and the opera, but in these latter days is rarely

seen at the Vienna places of amusement. He
has a positive liking for the details of government. The greater part of his day is spent in
official work. His favorite companions are his
political servants. He makes himself familiar
with every branch of administrative labor; perhaps there is no man in his dominions more
thoroughly conversant with their political and
social condition. When Count Von Beust, the
Protestant Saxon, became Chancellor of Austria,
it was the Emperor who "crammed" him on
the state of the realm, and instructed him in the
duties he had just assumed. His watchful eye
embraces the needs of all his subjects. Reign-
ing now under constitutional forms, there is yet
no doubt that there is no more weighty voice in
the Imperial councils than that of their chief
member. It was undoubtedly his personal influence, pitted against the general voice of his
advisers, that restrained Austria from going to
war in alliance with France against Prussia in
1870; and a very wise restraint it was.

Francis Joseph is one of the few great princes
of Europe against whom scandal has never
breathed a suspicion of immorality. From early
youth to the present hour his reputation has been

morally stainless. His life has been pure, simple, self-controlled. He has been a true and faithful husband to the most beautiful princess in Europe; a good, affectionate, and judicious father to children of whose promising qualities he has every reason to be proud. He told his son and heir, Rudolph, that he should never be compelled to marry for reasons of state, or to secure a brilliant alliance; but in the matter of marriage, should follow the inclinations of his own heart. The father himself had set this example. His union with the Princess Elizabeth of Bavaria was a love match, and brought Francis Joseph no other advantage than a happy and harmonious wedded life and domestic circle. The Emperor is abstemious and moderate, fond of simple food, and regular and methodical in his habits. He is little addicted to out-of-door sports, and is emphatically a "home body." So virtuous and clean a life is seldom to be found in palaces. Francis Joseph has waxed in popularity as his reign has lengthened, until now there is probably no living sovereign held more affectionately in the hearts of his subjects. His hand is always ready to give out of the abundance of his economically kept wealth in deeds of quiet charity. Truly, if the nations must still have hereditary rulers, and if their destinies must yet for a while be swayed somewhat by the accident of individual birth, theirs is good fortune to which that accident gives them such monarchs as now reign in Austria and Germany.

University Press: John Wilson & Son, Cambridge.